JULIEN SANDREL

Translated from the French by
Adriana Hunter

Quercus

First published in the French language as *La vie qui m'attendait*
by Éditions Calmann-Lévy, Paris, in 2019

First published in Great Britain in 2020 by Quercus
This paperback edition published in 2021 by

Quercus Editions Ltd
Carmelite House
50 Victoria Embankment
London EC4Y 0DZ

An Hachette UK company

A CIP catalogue record for this book is available
from the British Library

PB ISBN 978 1 52940 647 4
EB ISBN 978 1 52940 644 3

10 9 8 7 6 5 4 3 2 1

Typeset by Jouve (UK), Milton Keynes

Printed and bound in Great Britain by Clays Ltd, Elcograf S.p.A.

Papers used by Quercus are from well-managed forests
and other responsible sources.

The LIFE I WAS MEANT TO LIVE

Julien Sandrel was born in 1980 in the south of France, is married and has two children. His first novel, *The Book of Wonders*, was published in France by Calmann-Lévy in 2018. Rights to the novel sold in twenty-six territories; it was an international bestseller and is currently being adapted for film.

Also by Julien Sandrel

The Book of Wonders

To my parents.

To my brothers.

I meant to write about death, only
life came breaking in as usual.

Virginia Woolf

Can my whole life really come down to that one day?

It was the most beautiful, the most terrible, the most definitive day. Seminal yet destructive. Confronting me, in a sudden unbearable onslaught, with the incandescent breath of life and its exact opposite.

Oh, I lived that day. But I've never described it. Not to anyone.

And yet the memories are so vivid. Bitter. Brutal. But the wounds have healed over. Knitted together. It was a long time before I felt beauty was within my grasp again. Before it broke away from the unendurable images that I can't stop seeing every time I close my eyelids, however fleetingly.

To this day, my heart – and how could it do otherwise? – continues to hammer home the fact that I did what had to be done.

I'm sorry.

PART 1
Years

1

My life

'Yes, sir. I'll make sure it's done. My best wishes to your good lady wife.'

I put down the phone, amazed at myself. Does anyone else use that expression? It was already out of date last century.

I sound like an old woman, live like an old woman and only talk to old people. I *am* old. Old and lonely, that sums up my life.

But let's begin at the beginning.

My name is Romane, I'm thirty-nine and I'm a GP, specializing in hypochondria with paranoid tendencies. It's a niche specialization, but I apply it to myself alone – my patients can rest easy. More out of habit than choice, I live in Paris where I was born. I don't travel much, because I'm frightened of almost anything that can take you further than a ten-kilometre radius. Getting into a car is an ordeal. As for a train, a boat or a plane – let's not go there. I know the statistics: one crash for every twelve million flights, you're less likely to die in an aeroplane than to win the lottery. Well, I find that terrifying because there may not be many of them, but lottery winners definitely do exist. I also don't travel much because I'm frightened of spiders, snakes, anything that stings, bites or scratches, malaria, dengue, chikungunya, rabies, avian flu, being kidnapped by a mafia-like organization, having a heart attack a long way from a top-class hospital and dying of dehydration from a simple case of dysentery.

My panic attacks have been getting worse recently. To the point of obsession, some would say (including my psychiatrist). For six months now I've had bouts of what's called hyperventilation. The minute something stresses me, I have this sense of imminent danger and I have to breathe into a small paper bag to get it under control. Picture the scene in the fruit and veg aisle of my local supermarket: a woman sitting next to the courgettes, suffocating because her hand happened to alight on a mouldering piece of fruit, and she thinks she'll succumb to a hideous bacterial infection within the hour . . . that's me. I have the pleasure of morphing into a panting little dog several times a day, and Air France sick bags have become my most trusty companions. By an extraordinary twist of fate, my friend Melissa is an airline pilot, and she's become my official supplier.

Old, lonely, ridiculous and a hypochondriac.

I could add ugly, but to be honest, that's not true. I get

to see a lot of bodies every day, examining them with perfect safety thanks to my latex gloves, and I'm well aware that mine's not the worst. But I still can't help the fact that I don't like my body, so I hide it under bland clothes.

I'm discreet, almost invisible. That's what people like. People, not men. But then, the only man in my life is my father. I grew up with just him, protected by him, I've always followed the path he set out for me, and until six months ago I still lived with him. That's how much I love my father. It almost chokes me. My therapist says my hyperventilating is just a somatic manifestation of my need for air, to break away from my father. 'Wouldn't you say there's a disturbing connection between your breathing problems and your decision to move away from him?' he asked pointedly. He's probably right, particularly as the breathing hasn't got any better, despite the move. On the brink of turning forty, I decided to learn to live without my father. I cut the ties. My psychiatrist assures me it was a good decision, and it was high time.

It was high time, but it was late coming. Far too late for my father to accept it calmly. I have tried to tell him that normal people with normal lives see their parents three times a year, and call them once or twice a month, so we don't have to be so extreme, and yes, we can manage the transition from living under the same roof to different roofs, from constant surveillance of my every decision to a weekly phone call, and anyway it'll spare him long years of hormonal upheavals and assorted mood swings . . . so he should be grateful, shouldn't he? No, of course not. As far as my father's concerned, this radical change in our daily lives is both incomprehensible and unacceptable.

For a few months now he's only talked to me when he absolutely had to. It sometimes feels as if I'm dealing with a sulking sixty-five-year-old child who's disappointed because he's lost his favourite toy. His reaction hurt me at first – it was too harsh, too drastic – but then I got used to it. I actually think this temporary distance is what's needed, it's doing us both good. It'll take time for my father to accept the new situation, but he'll get there. Once he's over the shock, our relationship will be more normal. More regular. And so will my breathing.

I've just realized that I'm talking about this like a lover's break-up. *You're in really bad shape, girl. This is your father, there's no break-up, this is a healthy move away. Breathe, Romane. Breathe.*

Old, lonely, hypochondriac, pathetic, but I can heal myself. Or at least I'm trying.

*

After ending the call with my patient I allow myself a few minutes to have a glass of water and freshen up my face. It's a blisteringly hot day and I have the unpleasant impression I'm in a hammam, minus the massage and the Middle Eastern pastries. I'm keeping my little paper bag within reach because the humidity is oppressive. My clothes cling to me, my patients cling to me, my gloves cling to me. On the radio this morning they said it would get to thirty-eight degrees. A record in Paris, even for the 15th of July. I've booked some time off at the end of the week and I still don't know what I'm going to do. Nothing scares me more than ending up on my own – and God knows I'm scared of enough things. But I do have to take this time off: Paris empties significantly at this time of year, so keeping the surgery open doesn't make any sense. As motivation to get out of this oven of a capital, I keep telling myself that having some rest is bound to bolster my immune system. At least there's that.

Flippedy flip, it's hot! Yes, that's how I talk. In my head I'm saying, *Fuck, I can't fucking take this shit-hole heat*, but the idea dissolves before it passes my lips. I've bought a fan for the surgery, and one for my bedroom. Last night – thanks to the Bastille Day celebrations – I hardly slept at all. With my windows open, I heard the drink-fuelled altercations of the local soaks, and couldn't help imagining some individual with unsavoury intentions looming into view at any moment. Even though I live on the fifth floor, so unless Spiderman has an evil twin, the risk of intruders is pretty limited. All the same, I couldn't relax. I woke dripping with sweat several times. Which means people had better not push me too far today. That's what I think to myself – like I'd actually clobber anyone who wound me up. As if. The truth is, I'm the same today as every other day: agonizingly polite.

I peel my blouse away from my back one last time and open the door. Madame Lebrun – seventy years old, such black hair it's getting worrying and such perfect teeth they're getting suspect – steps into my office.

She's been a patient a long time and, according to my father, she's an acquaintance of his: I know he saw her regularly when he worked as a park-keeper at Buttes-Chaumont. At one point I suspected they knew each other much better than they admitted.

Madame Lebrun, normally such a talkative woman, sits down without a word. I'm amazed by her silence. Worried by it.

'Romane, dear, we need to talk, you and I.'

Madame Lebrun peers at me with her small dark eyes. She's clutching her handbag on her knee, her face is unreadable. She's never looked at me like this.

I don't know this yet, but Madame Lebrun is about to change the course of my life.

In a few minutes' time, nothing will be the same again. Ever.

2

I'm fine

Madame Lebrun is always clear, distinct, precise. *It's my personality, you know what I'm like, Romane, dear.* I certainly know her well enough to be sure she always means well. Not the sort to spread gossip or freight her words with hidden meaning regardless of the consequences. So when she asks cautiously if everything's OK, it makes me shudder. My body tenses.

'Of course everything's OK. But I'm the doctor around here, *I* should be asking *you*. What brings you here?' I ask, trying to hide my anxiety behind forced jollity. Madame Lebrun takes a deep breath and looks me in the eye.

'I won't beat about the bush, Romane, dear. You know how fond I am of you. You know I don't have any children and . . . and I've always thought of you as . . . important.'

Pause. Too long a pause. My paranoid nutcase tendencies nudge me towards thinking the worst. Madame Lebrun is going to give me terrible news; Madame Lebrun is dying. She looks perfectly healthy but I know just how sneaky illness can be.

'I was in Marseilles last weekend, Romane.'

What can your little trip to Marseilles possibly mean to me? I think, but I obviously don't say anything.

'My sister's broken her hip,' she continues. 'I went to visit her. She's in hospital, the Hôpital Nord.'

'I'm so sorry to hear that. I'm sure everything will sort itself out soon enough. She's still young, I seem to remember. You mustn't wor–'

'My sister isn't the problem, Romane, she'll recover. *You're* the problem.'

Did she just interrupt me abruptly? That's not like her at all.

'I'm not sure I'm following this . . . What problem do you mean?'

'I saw you, Romane. In Marseilles. I nipped down to buy a magazine in the hospital shop and I saw you come in.'

Flippedy flip, Madame Lebrun's lost the plot.

'I was intrigued because your father hadn't said anything about you going there, but mostly . . .'

'Mostly what?'

'Mostly . . . because you were in disguise. You'd put on a red wig and a dress that was a bit too low cut to my mind, but well, it's the sort of thing people wear these days. So I followed you, without a word. I wanted to know.'

'What are you talking about, Madame Lebrun? I've never been to Marseilles in my life, and I stayed at home last Saturday binge-watching an American TV series. You saw someone who looked like me and you came up with some improbable scenario, that's all . . . How are you feeling? Are you having headaches at all?'

'Romane, dear, don't make fun of me. I may be old but I'm not stupid. I'm very well, thank you, and I'd like to be able to say the same of you . . . I just wanted to remind you that . . . if you need anything, I'm here. I haven't breathed a word to your father, of course. My lips are sealed.'

She seems to be genuinely upset, worried about me.

'This is ridiculous. I don't know what sort of story you've whipped up about me but I can assure you I'm absolutely fine. Stop fretting about me, I get plenty of that from my father.'

'But, Romane, I saw you, for goodness' sake! At the other end of the country, so no one would know. I followed you, I saw the doctor show you into his office. I saw the serious expression on his face, I saw you coughing. I waited for you and half an hour later you came out with your file under your arm, and you burst into tears. You put sunglasses on to hide the state you were in. You looked dazed but you hurried away. I went over to the doctor's door and on the door it said . . .'

I don't understand a word of what Madame Lebrun is

saying. I can feel a panic attack coming on, my breathing's accelerating. She notices, gets to her feet and puts a hand on my shoulder. She hesitates for a moment, then makes up her mind to challenge me.

'Romane, why did you see the head of pulmonology at the Hôpital Nord?'

*

After that I lost track of the conversation. My mind went into limbo.

Madame Lebrun put so much effort into persuading me that I really was ill that I gave up trying to contradict her. I needed to get her out of my consulting room, and quickly. The heat was catching at my throat. I was suffocating. I needed to breathe into my little bag but I didn't want to do it in front of her, I didn't want to encourage her bonkers hypotheses with concrete actions and images. I thanked her and she promised, again, that she wouldn't say anything to my father, it would be just between the two of us. She reiterated her support and I shovelled her towards the exit.

Once the door was closed, I sat on the floor, and it took a good ten minutes to settle my breathing.

I dealt with the next four consultations in under an hour and cut short the day. I couldn't concentrate and needed to get home. To think.

Madame Lebrun saw a distressed woman who wasn't

me, because I know perfectly well where I was last Saturday. Flippedy flip, that crazy old woman's putting the weirdest words in my mouth – it wasn't me, end of story, I don't need to add justifications. But Madame Lebrun isn't crazy, that's the point. Her conviction has got to me because she seemed to be in full possession of her faculties. One detail of her story gets to me more than all the rest of it: she mentioned a red wig. I've had brown hair since my teens, but red is my natural colour. I don't think Madame Lebrun has ever seen me with red hair. Obviously, I'm not the only redhead on the planet, and of course my father could have mentioned my colouring. *It's a coincidence or a pack of lies, that's all, Romane.*

The way my mind has concentrated on the colour of this Marseilles woman's hair over the course of the evening has allowed a hypothesis to emerge gradually. And it's as whacky as it's exciting. What if she's a member of my family? That would explain the vague similarity. What if Madame Lebrun's curiosity was finally giving me an opportunity to meet one of the relatives my father always refuses to talk about, having cut off all ties with them after Mum died?

My mother's death. The event – I'm convinced of this – that provoked my weaknesses, my fears, my father's fears, my isolation, my co-dependent relationship with him that's so hard to escape, my life . . . my absence of life.

My mother died when I'd just turned one.

In the most tragic way – saving me.

I have absolutely no memories of her, or of that winter afternoon. Could there be impressions and sensations imprinted somewhere in the convolutions of my brain? Nothing conscious, anyway. I was so young.

My father has always told me it was a beautiful day. It was the least you could ask, 'for a goddess's last day'. It couldn't fail to be. So I've always had an irrational aversion for sunshine on crisp, cold days. Those rays of light are blades that cut right through me and endlessly reflect my mother's death. And even though my father has always insisted fatalistically that it couldn't be helped, that 'it was nobody's fault, just bad luck', I've always felt responsible. She gave her life for me. If she hadn't lunged to push the buggy onto the pavement, *I* would have died. My psychiatrist now sweeps aside this searing guilt with a flick of his hand. After all these years of therapy I need to move on. But I just can't. When I look at photos of Mum, she's so smiley, so beautiful, so much *better than me*, I can't help feeling her life deserved to go on longer.

My father concentrated all his hopes, all his attention and all his love on me. That's why it's so difficult for me to break away completely. We've always been a family of two. My father's turned the page on the past, scrupulously. I've never met so much as a great-uncle, not one great-aunt, no one, ever.

And now, out of the blue, Madame Lebrun is offering me a new possibility. A different outlook. It's probably unfounded, but who knows? I must have some distant cousins, I wasn't conceived by the Holy Spirit, despite my parents' names: Mary and Joseph. I've always thought that if I'd been a boy, they'd have called me Jesus . . . so that was a narrow escape.

But that's another story. Let's get back to what I've been obsessing about since Madame Lebrun's revelation: I want to meet this woman. I need to know. To be sure one way or the other.

I'm lying on my bed but sleep is out of the question.

Madame Lebrun has needled me. She's stirred up something in me that goes way beyond curiosity. She was so sure of herself, so sure she'd seen *me*, it's worrying. And exhilarating. How long is it since something this exciting has happened to me? I try to gather my thoughts; they're pinging off in every direction. Some of them morbid. Most of them intoxicating.

Two in the morning, I'm still not asleep.

I go back over what Madame Lebrun said, fast-forwarding it, rewinding it and playing it in slo-mo in my mind.

It's unbearably hot in my apartment. I decide to have

another shower. A cold one. The icy water jets into my face and I suddenly know what to do. I race out of the bathroom with a towel knotted around my chest. I'm still soaking but who cares.

It's the middle of July, I'll be off work in three days' time and I still don't have any plans. I'm free as a sea breeze, and surely one of those would do me the world of good. I'll go to Marseilles. Really explore this city I've never set foot in.

I turn on my computer and start organizing my holiday. Frenetically.

I don't think I've been this excited for a long time.

I'll see the rugged Calanques cliffs, the Canebière high street, the city's oldest 'Panier' quarter, the modernist Cité Radieuse . . .

And the Hôpital Nord.

3

Marseilles

I alight at the city's Saint-Charles station and am hit by the stifling heat. Having shivered for three hours in a carriage with too much air con, the contrast is almost painful. I thought this intensity of heat only happened in places far inland, but it turns out it's just as punishing on the shores of the Mediterranean.

I'm relieved the train arrived without incident. I took a muscle relaxant just before it set off, thinking this would help me drift off to sleep. Well, that wasn't happening – the train was overflowing with children whizzing about in every direction. I had plenty of time to imagine scenarios of major rail disasters, jumping almost out of my seat every time we hurtled into a tunnel. I'm far happier confronting the scorching Marseilles air, with my feet firmly on the ground.

The whole area around the station is swarming with families, bulging suitcases and exuberant gangs of teenagers enjoying the monitored freedom of summer camps that they'll look back on fondly – or not, if like me they shudder at the thought of showering surrounded by their fellow campers' pubic hair. It's Saturday, 18 July, one of the peak dates to set off on holiday in France. I hadn't appreciated the full horror of this, or I'd have thought twice and deferred leaving for a couple of days. But here I am.

As I elbow my way to the taxi queue, I hear a volley of abuse coming from a black saloon with tinted windows: an Uber driver is treated to a selection of the most handsome local insults, reinforced by delightful gestures. I can't help smiling to think I'm in Marseilles, a city that the media caricatured as dangerous, dirty and abandoned for a long time. In the last few years I've seen a flurry of articles about its beautiful scenery and its cultural revival. I'm in Marseilles and I'm delighted. I formulate this thought clearly, and the fact that I've applied that simple adjective – delighted – to myself is sufficiently rare to be worth mentioning.

I've allowed myself a little extravagance . . . well, if I'm going to have a holiday, I might as well book myself an amazing room. So I chose a recently renovated luxury hotel with giddying views down over the old port, the big wheel and the Basilica of Notre-Dame de la Garde. The place is incredible, the view breathtaking and the temperature in my sumptuous room perfect. I catch myself smiling. Trying to imagine what my life would be like if I lived here, in the far south of France. Would the pace of things be the same? Would my everyday life be easier? I could spend hours gazing at the views. I *could*, but that's not what's going to happen, not at all.

In theory, I've set aside the weekend to relax and rest, waiting till Monday before I go to the Hôpital Nord. As if this really were a holiday. But of course, that's not what I want now. Did I ever really think I would? All my resolutions went out of the window as soon as I set foot on Marseilles soil. I might as well be honest with myself: I came here with one clear aim, and I'll never make it through a whole weekend without thinking about this woman who I have been obsessed with for three full days. I get changed, knot a plain grey scarf in my hair, spritz myself with perfume, try to make myself as presentable as possible, deem that I've done OK and set off down the steps of my magnificent hotel. I've got my stash of little paper bags with me but I haven't used a single one since arriving in Marseilles. I hail a taxi and, feverish with excitement, head towards the north of the city.

A stark change of scenery. Rows of low-rise buildings, grim concrete. In amongst all this, though, there's a bubbly, cliché-defying atmosphere of happy hardworking people. The charming driver runs out of superlatives singing the praises of his city and tells me how unbelievably lucky I am to be discovering it, seeing it for the first time. He drops me outside the hospital, which looks exactly like the residential tower blocks all around it, but even here the cicadas sing deafeningly. It's no lie, these insects chirp the whole time, giving a touch of sun-kissed charm to places that are cruelly lacking any of their own. It's the first time I've heard them sing for real, not in a film, and I think it's beautiful, and moving.

Once inside the building I spot the shop in the main concourse and find I'm looking out for Madame Lebrun. Obviously, this is absurd, but I know intuitively that she's just the sort to carry on watching me until I've admitted that I'm ill. I go over to reception and ask where the pulmonology department is, thank you madame, have a nice day madame.

One hospital is really very like another: the same frenzied activity everywhere, the same strained faces. Hospitals are short of funding; time is too rare a commodity for all these men and women who devote their days and nights to comforting, saving and improving whoever and whatever they can. I admire them and I resent the political leaders who sit on their hands, always give in to the power of finances, and do nothing to improve the working conditions of thousands of medical staff, and the living conditions of thousands of patients. Even though good health is the first thing we all want for our loved ones, and the most wonderful of gifts. But good health is becoming a luxury. It makes me sick.

After I qualified as a doctor, I decided to focus on what's known as 'general practice' (words that are sometimes said with a whiff of contempt, an implication of inferiority in comparison with 'real' medicine, the sort that goes on in university hospitals). I personally think they're two sides of the same coin. Complementary, indispensable. I'm far too aware of human suffering not to take the time to listen. So I sit there in my little consulting room and listen. I'm one of those doctors who favours quality over quantity. At least, I try to.

The pulmonology department is buzzing with people. I hang around the admissions desk for a while, trying to find the waiting room. I don't have a plan of attack, nothing. Well, actually, I have a very simple game plan – I'm going to sit and watch. I know that patients always have their own habits: some call my office several weeks in advance to be sure they'll get that slot at 8.30 on a Monday morning, and when I ask them why they're so keen on that slot, they invariably say that it's just theirs, end of story. So I'm thinking Saturday may be the chosen hospital appointment day of this woman who looks so like me. I've got my iPad with me, the department is air conditioned, and I have all the time in the world. If nothing happens today, then I'll think again.

I'm about to sit down when a young medical secretary waves me over to the desk. I suddenly feel slightly shaky. What does she want?

'That's lucky, I thought you'd already left the building. You forgot your social security card after your appointment earlier. Here. Enjoy the rest of the day.'

I mumble some thanks, turn around, pause, then hurry off, clutching the card I've just been given. My heartbeats reverberate right into my limbs. It's perfectly obvious what's just happened: the young secretary mistook me for the woman I'm looking for. She didn't have a moment's hesitation. So Madame Lebrun's not the only one; we must be very alike. I wasn't expecting such instant progress.

I can feel a dizzy spell coming on. My breathing's getting choppy – I'm a thief on the run. I glance around furtively; it feels like everyone knows I've stolen someone else's health insurance card. I think I can see disapproving looks. I'm walking quickly, very quickly. I still haven't looked at the card in my hand, and I really hope it's the new kind, with a photo. I'm just about to see this face which is apparently so like mine.

I come out of the building and slump down onto a low wall, near a couple of ambulancemen having a cigarette break. I take out my best paper bag and bring it up to my mouth, while they watch with some embarrassment. They stub out their cigarettes and cut short their break; I feel bad for driving them away, I hadn't thought of that. I hadn't thought of anything much, to be honest. I wish I could be tiny, disappear down a mouse hole, but I need to sit here and catch my breath. Then I can look at the card.

I count one, two, three . . . then look at it.

Shit shit shit shit. It's one of the old ones, without a photo. I scan it for a name: Juliette Delgrange. Totally unrelated to my father's name, or my mother's. A nice name but it's nothing to do with me. I'm disappointed. The soufflé collapses. Any hope that this woman is a distant relation is fading. My breathing goes back to normal. I'm annoyed with myself for being so naive, annoyed with myself for thinking something even remotely interesting could happen to me.

I automatically read the sequence of impersonal numbers on the smart card and, all at once, some of my deadened neurones fire up again.

I shudder. These health cards aren't like other cards. The first few numbers are coded to indicate the holder's gender, year of birth, date of birth and region of birth. I'm terribly thirsty and can't concentrate any more. I run over to the nearest drinks machine, gulp down a whole bottle of water, gather my wits and peer at the card till my eyes ache.

The first seven numbers of Juliette Delgrange's health card tell me that she's a woman born in Paris in January 1976.

Like me.

[illegible] code, but I need [illegible] here and [illegible]
[illegible]

[illegible]

[illegible] what [illegible] one [illegible]
[illegible] I [illegible] really
[illegible] my father's [illegible] my mother [illegible]
[illegible]
The [illegible] Any [illegible] this [illegible]
[illegible] is [illegible] going back
[illegible] for [illegible]
[illegible] sometimes even
[illegible] happen [illegible]

[illegible] read the [illegible]
numbers on the smart card and, all at once, some of my
[illegible]

[illegible] These [illegible] cards [illegible]
The first [illegible]
[illegible] of birth [illegible]
[illegible]
[illegible] to the [illegible] only
[illegible] my [illegible]
[illegible]

The [illegible] gave [illegible]
card [illegible]
[illegible]

I [illegible]

4

Impossible

I stay sitting on that wall for a long time, reeling. A male nurse asks me if I've got a light and tries to strike up conversation. I show him my little paper bag and pretend I don't speak French. He doesn't believe me but gets the message. I sit there, staring straight ahead, not seeing a thing. Shaken to the core.

On the way back to the hotel I find out as much as I can about this Juliette Delgrange who's become astonishingly real now that she has a name. What I want more than anything else is to find a picture of her. To see her with my own eyes.

The search engine on my smartphone leads me straight to Facebook. There are three Juliette Delgranges. I'm not on Facebook myself – for obvious reasons of personal safety – so I can only see their profile pictures. Which is plenty as a starting point. I click on the first profile, feeling the blood pounding in my temples. A photo appears. Nothing like me. At least, I hope no one would confuse me with this monster, that would be a blow to morale . . . Yes, I can be a bitch sometimes – but it goes without saying, it all stays inside my head. The second profile doesn't have an image, which is super rare these days. I'm worried it's her, but she's quite right to protect herself, the web's riddled with every sort of pervert.

I try the third profile. The last one. My right hand's shaking like a leaf so I steady my phone with my left hand, wedging my arm against the door. The image takes a long, long time to appear. I'm in a taxi, the signal on my phone is unreliable. I pin all my hopes on the screen. For a moment, I picture myself as a child, at night, in all the expectation of the presidential elections. The new president's face appears slowly on our cumbersome old TV, from the top down, spinning out the suspense for thousands of half-wonderstruck, half-infuriated viewers. At this precise moment, in this taxi that's travelling far too quickly, I'm kept on tenterhooks as Juliette Delgrange is revealed millimetre by millimetre.

When her face appears, I cry out, bring my hand to my mouth and burst into uncontrollable tears. I turn the phone away, as if the image could hurt me. I let that first shock consume me for a moment, sitting in silence, with my eyes closed. Then I look at the picture again, zooming in and analysing it in detail. How's this possible?

The photo's slightly out of focus, at an angle, probably not the best one there is of her. I don't trust images: every ugly duckling can be turned into a sex symbol in three seconds flat these days. Filters distort the colours, alter reality. But Juliette Delgrange's face is incredibly like mine. Her hair does look red, there's no doubt about that. A red that's so familiar to me. The thick, dense texture of her hair looks similar too. I can't see the colour of her eyes because of the angle. Mine are blue, a blue that I've always thought hard, making the rest of my face bland. And my face itself is too white, smattered with freckles so that I've always looked like a poor man's Emma Stone. At school they sometimes nicknamed me 'Freckle' or 'Carrot-top'. Was Juliette Delgrange taunted like this? Did she cope with it better?

I can't take my eyes off her face. I think it's beautiful. With a natural, obvious beauty. I've never seen myself as attractive, I've always thought I have no charm of any sort. How come I see her so differently when we're this alike? What's altered my perception so drastically? The distance, the fact that it's not me, of course. But not just that. In this photo, Juliette Delgrange has an aura, a charisma that I've never had, and never will. She's smiling, she looks happy, sure of herself. She looks as if she *feels* beautiful. And that changes everything.

The driver – who's nothing like as friendly as the

previous one – is very worried I'll 'trash the leather seats' when I take out my Air France bag. I can understand he's worried about customers puking, given the quantity of artificial vanilla fragrance polluting the inside of his Mercedes. I reassure him that I'm only going to breathe into it so he needn't worry. He glances at me in the rear-view mirror, probably thinking I should be locked up. True, in the last five minutes I've screamed, cried and panted like a dog. He might have a point.

I carry on with my research, and in a dozen clicks I've got a good idea of Juliette Delgrange's life: I've identified her job, where she lives, some of her hobbies – the things that she agrees, willingly or not, to make public. It's amazing what the Internet can tell you about a stranger in the space of twenty little minutes.

Juliette Delgrange owns a bookshop in the middle of Avignon, with a rudimentary website: an address and a picture of the pretty old-fashioned shopfront, A Word from Juliette. An irregular-shaped wooden sign covered in slightly peeling, soft-green paint, with the name of the shop picked out in white letters in fine schoolgirl writing, a few flowers in front of the door. A place that gives off an instant feeling of extraordinary serenity, of poetry. I try to find a picture of the owner, but there isn't one.

Twitter helps me complete the virtual portrait of Juliette Delgrange. She's crazy about books – well, I'd got that – and theatre. Her account is full of tweets with news and comments on shows, a few recommendations for 'unmissable' plays, and some succinct advice about the raft of new novels that came out in the spring. No new photo of her, I'll have to make do with what I have.

And that's more than enough to leave me seriously shaken.

*

Back at the hotel, I negotiate fiercely to pay for just one night instead of the seven I booked. They agree – it *is* the middle of July and the hotel's full, it won't be difficult for them to fill the room and I genuinely look traumatized by the 'personal problem' that's come up and means I must leave Marseilles immediately. I make my way back to Saint-Charles station and hop on a high-speed train, only hours after alighting from one.

My time in Marseilles was short-lived. Less than a day – a record. I promise myself I'll come back, in better circumstances. Marseilles is a seductress, an unusual, sensual place. Its sharp blue skies amplified the impact of my discoveries, its music heightened my feelings in a way I could never have imagined.

*

I spend most of my journey looking for somewhere to stay, desperately grateful to have at my disposal electronic gadgets that mean even the most disorganized people can find somewhere to put a roof over their heads at the eleventh hour.

I arrive in Avignon at twelve minutes past eight on a Saturday evening in July in a heatwave. The streets are seething with people, restaurants spill far beyond the limits of their terraces, and there's noisy, exuberant bustle all around. The place is in full party mode. I realize I've arrived in the middle of the famous theatre festival. Every year I'm bored by endless reports giving me an enthusiastic injection of culture, and encouraging me to join in the greatest theatre event of the year. Avignon claims it's 'the biggest theatre in the world', with buildings all over the city pressed into service as theatres during the festival month. With its 1,500 shows it generates over a million admissions in the last three weeks of July. Hell on earth for an agoraphobic.

I slalom laboriously towards the small studio I managed to track down at the last minute, dragging my noisy suitcase behind me, and trying to find my way using the supposedly intelligible map on my smartphone. In a cobbled street the wheels twist awkwardly and my bag rolls over. I glance over my shoulder, embarrassed. I catch a whiff of rising sweat, surreptitiously check an armpit, assess that I'm the culprit and promise I'll apply more deodorant as soon as possible, then set off again, going through the whole rolled-over suitcase performance at least ten times. I come very close to crying and giving up, but I'm so near my goal: Juliette Delgrange's bookshop is only a few streets away. I can't stop, not now, the cogs have been set in motion. Inside my head, in my guts, right there, deep down.

I get the keys to the studio from a small box screwed to the door, only protected by a four-figure code – it all strikes me as terribly reckless: I can just imagine what would happen if someone had had a copy made of the keys and was waiting for me up there with ropes, a knife, a chainsaw, who knows. I try to block out the images, climb the two flights of stairs and open the door with my heart pounding. No bloodthirsty murderers. I double-lock the door and rush to the shower. God, that feels good. This seems to be all I do at the moment: sweat, suffocate, shudder, have showers . . .

The studio is small but well laid-out, furnished 100 per cent by IKEA, clean, almost cosy. I turn on the fan and settle into a rocking chair – one of the Swedish giant's bestsellers. I close my eyes; I need some calm so that I can go back over all the theories whirring around in my brain, exhausting me.

Who is Juliette Delgrange?

Theory 1 (the most probable): she's a dead ringer. Someone who looks like me and who may not actually be a natural redhead, who's not connected in any way to me, or to Emma Stone.

Theory 2: Juliette Delgrange is a distant cousin. That's an option I've considered from the start and it's still there. If it turns out to be right, then I'll need a major explanation from my father about how we're related because I don't know of anyone called Delgrange in my family. As I'm working through this theory, it dawns on me that Delgrange may not be her maiden name, it may be her married name. Of course, how did I not think of this before? Not everyone has to be as lonely as I am. This thought makes me sad but puts the unknown cousin scenario right back in pole position.

Basically, there aren't any other theories for people in their right mind.

But there are for me.

I'm on my old hobbyhorse about probabilities, lottery winners who've got their hands on an *impossible* gold mine, and people who die in *impossible* plane crashes.

Two women born in the same month, in the same year, in the same city. Two women who look *impossibly* alike.

No one ever believes the impossible. Except the people who live through it, or die by it.

Theory 3: The *impossible* theory.

It's impossible, of course. It's impossible by definition. That's what I keep telling myself. The implications of this scenario are far too painful. I'm not sure I can or even want to deal with them. I think I'm losing my mind, I can't sleep, I'm forgetting to breathe. I'm having one of the toughest nights of my life. A night spent holding my breath.

The zero probability is gradually erased. The theory corrupts every tiny corner of my brain. Becomes a bulky cyst. A tumour. And my body's starting to give it a dangerous amount of space.

Because I'm consumed by the strange beauty of it.

Now I can breathe. I fall asleep.

5

Juliette

I'm getting more and more tired; the last few nights have been gruelling. I've never been a big sleeper but right now I'm managing an average of four hours a night, and that's not enough. I've got five-metre bags under my eyes and I do my best to camouflage them. It was still twenty-seven degrees in the middle of the night in my Avignon studio so I opened the windows and I'm now a constellation of mosquito bites. Luckily, my face was spared, so I won't look like a pre-teen having a hormone surge.

I head out at 9.30, putting the keys to the studio back in their little coded box. It's Sunday, but the bookshop's website says that the shop is open seven days a week during the festival. I wonder how Juliette managed to go to Marseilles yesterday. Does she have employees? A partner? I also wonder whether she realizes she's lost her health insurance card. Has she been in touch with the hospital? Did she have a row over the phone with the secretary? 'But I gave you back your card myself, what are you implying?'

I run through all these inoffensive notions again and again to avoid being overwhelmed by other, more meaningful thoughts. There's no point losing myself in conjecture, I just need to go and see her. What on earth can I say? 'Hello, you don't know me but we do have a family resemblance, wouldn't you say? By the way, I know you're ill, I've stolen your health card, stalked you from Marseilles . . . that all makes me look like a dangerous psychopath but I do hope you won't run away.' Whatever I say and whatever I do, she'll think I'm mad anyway, so I might as well stop ruminating over it.

I've already tortured myself enough about what the *impossible* theory could imply. The first and most obvious thing is a lie. A lie that's gone on for nearly forty years, and that's a big deal. So it can't be that, I refuse to contemplate it. Here's what's going to happen: I'll get a close look, this Juliette will turn out to be a fake redhead with brownish eyes, a much bigger nose than in the photo (which was probably photoshopped), a few crooked teeth and a huge mole on her forehead. I'll say hello, give her back her health card, saying I was mistaken for her at the hospital yesterday – ha ha, that's a joke, isn't it, I can't see it either – and I was on my way to Avignon so I offered to give it back to her and here it is, no, don't thank me, you're welcome, it was only natural, goodbye, lovely to have met you, and by the way, here are the contact details of a good dermatologist, you should have that mole looked at some time.

By the time I've finished a few of these imaginary conversations, I'm already outside the bookshop. Avignon isn't Paris, the distances are appreciably shorter. The shop opens at ten, so I sit on a bench on the pavement opposite and watch the comings and goings in the street. It's still early but the city is already buzzing. A group of actors and jugglers appear, singing the praises of their show this evening, backed by loud music like in a circus performance. I have front-row seats. One of the jugglers, dressed as a clown, comes over and identifies me as easy prey. All eyes focus on me. I protest vigorously, I hate being the centre of attention. *What does this fucking clown want from me?* That's what I'm thinking inside my head, obviously. In real life, I smile stupidly, to the amusement of passers-by, and find myself recruited into the show, throwing skittles at a man dressed up as the sun with a Milky Way hat and a few planets bobbing around his face – the dick. I keep smiling but gesture to him that that's enough now, I was fine as I was. I hand back his skittles and he raises my arm in salute to him – I hope I'm not sweating already . . . no, all good. Loud applause from the delighted audience, and now the guy's trying to *mwah-mwah* my cheeks! At this point, I step aside meekly, remove myself from the performance as discreetly as possible and back away from the ring of gawping onlookers.

I keep backing away and flatten myself against a shopfront, with my eyes still pinned on the now retreating troupe. The chill of the window does me good. I take a deep breath. The guy dressed as the sun gives me a little wave and a smile . . . which I don't reciprocate. I check my watch: 9.50. The bookshop will be open soon. I look up, trying to work out where it is, and realize I've actually been leaning against the shop window of A Word from Juliette for the last few minutes.

I turn around, bridge my hands above my eyes, leaning against the window, and narrow my eyelids to get used to the darkness inside the shop. It takes my eyes a few seconds to adjust and the first thing they alight on is the back of the shop. I can see large polished bookcases in warm-coloured solid wood and two leather chairs with deep buttoning framing a mosaic-topped coffee table on which there are a number of beautiful books of black-and-white photographs. A shiver runs down my spine. Juliette Delgrange likes romantic interiors, clearly.

I continue my exploration, shifting my gaze slightly to the right, then peel my hand away from the window and take another step back.

I flinch. She's there.

Standing in front of me.

Looking at me. Frozen.

I can feel the flow of blood reaching every corner of my brain. My breathing accelerates. My legs start to shake.

Her eyes . . . everything imaginable flits across her eyes: fear, surprise, incredulity, death, life. Her right arm hangs limply by her side, a few books lie on the floor. Her left hand is bent across her chest, holding some books she was about to put on display. But something stopped her in her tracks.

In a split second I construct, conjure the scene from her point of view. The shop will be opening soon, Juliette needs to set up some bestsellers on the table by the door. She comes forward, notices the circus show in the street, and smiles, her attention momentarily caught by the clown. But also by the woman on the other side of the street. At first it's just a vague impression, a hint. Still, it's strange. She comes over to the window, looks more closely. She can't understand what she's seeing. It's her but not her. Another her. The embarrassment on this other her's face, the awkwardness in her gestures, the discretion bordering on complete self-effacement. But this woman's so like her, this woman who's pretending to enjoy being co-opted into a bit of street theatre, this woman who – she can tell, she can *feel* – wants to get away, and hide. She can't believe it at first. Well, how could she believe it? But this woman's right there before her eyes. She drops the books on the floor, doesn't notice. She starts to cry softly, alone in her bookshop. Her whole life, all her suffering and problems, it all rises up inside her. She stands transfixed by the shop window, and watches this unlikely stranger back towards her, lean against the window and catch her breath. She waits for this other her to turn around, to look her in the eye.

I am this other woman and I read all this in Juliette's eyes.

Her eyes are so vivid . . . they're all I can see. Set in the same white face smattered with the same freckles, piercing right through me with that fearsome blue. The same colour that I find so washed-out in myself looks beautiful and razor-sharp on her.

She can't stop looking at me. God, it can't be happening. Our eyes – yes, them again – are saying the same thing. They've understood before the rest of our bodies.

I can't hear any of the background hubbub now. All I can feel is towering fear, and towering joy.

Tears roll silently over her cheeks. I step closer. I press my hand to the window. She steps closer. She presses her hand to the window. I start to cry too. The moment lasts, stretches – sublime and warm and bewitching.

And then it happens, right there, just like that. She smiles at me. She smiles at me, crying at the same time. It's appalling and it's beautiful. And it's unbelievably powerful. I'm having real trouble breathing but I couldn't care less. Her lips open to reveal her teeth and it gets worse, it intensifies, it's confirmed. It's becoming unbearable. What I'm seeing goes far beyond anything I've imagined; all my theories are obsolete now, and there's no room for any doubt. I hadn't thought of this, I hadn't thought about her teeth, about that tooth. It's all I can see now, that little canine, tiny, microscopic, almost invisible. This unique characteristic of mine. Unique means there's only one of them. It means me and me alone. Not her. And yet . . . the tears which, up till now, have been a gentle patter, suddenly hit me in a powerful wave, submerging me.

Juliette moves towards the entrance. She wants to come and meet me but stops. I know instinctively that something's wrong. Despite my tear-filled eyes, I can see her reach to hold on to the pale wooden counter and cough, for a long time. A hoarse, hacking cough that I hear clearly even with the window between us. I feel her pain. I feel my own pain.

Is what I'm experiencing real? Despite my more than fertile imagination, I never pictured this. I don't understand, or rather I won't acknowledge what I understand only too well. Her reaction makes it clear that she didn't know either, she had no idea about any of this either.

She straightens again, looks at me, smiles and then looks away, almost shyly. She takes some keys from the pocket of her jeans and opens the door wide. I walk into the shop. Religiously. I can feel my heart tearing in two inside my chest. I step towards her and, stupidly, I hold out my hand to her – that's how you greet a stranger. She bursts out laughing and asks me to wait a moment. I watch her, dazed. Her laugh, her voice. I know them from family videos of my father's. I don't like them, I'm used to hearing them from inside myself. But I'm absolutely sure that this voice and this laugh are mine. I lean against a bookcase, overwhelmed. She puts on the lights in the shop and closes the curtain, so we can have some privacy, some time to ourselves. I don't think she'll open up the shop today after all. She's so beautiful.

We don't talk but our eyes are enough. They're laughing. Crying. Grasping what's going on, right in front of us, and it's not a game, it means too much. We both know the door that's opened will stir up a lot of secrets and pain, a lot of turmoil that neither of us could have imagined until now. We both also know that this door can never be closed again.

We look at each other.

There's already a 'we'.

We hesitate one last moment. One last vestige of restraint. One last distance between us.

Then she throws herself at me, and I let her.

Then I hug her to me, and she lets me.

My sister. My twin.

6

In the beginning

Juliette soon takes me home to her apartment above the shop. She dashes off a notice saying that, due to unforeseen circumstances, the shop will be closed today, Sunday, 19 July 2015. Then we spend the day together. Seven hours, to be precise. Seven hours to describe our lives – it's so little time. Frustration tinges our excitement, our urgent need to know everything about each other. Our urgent need to understand.

I'm really struck by the incredible intimacy established between us in the space of a few minutes. We can't stop touching each other, as if this physical contact were indispensable, as if to check this other me is really there, and real. I don't immediately register the reckless proximity I allow myself to her, I don't notice my complete absence of inhibition. And to think I'd normally have a whole internal debate before touching a stranger, always frightened I'll be contaminated by some foul miasma, but even though I know that she's ill and I have no idea whether her condition is contagious,

I don't even think about protecting myself. As if blood ties are stronger than any of that. As if touching her is more important. It's true, it is.

From the start, we're in no doubt: we must be twins. The resemblance is too striking; we're virtually identical, down to the tiniest detail: the same height, the same weight (give or take a kilo, in her favour), the same eyes, the same smile even though it's so distinctive, the same hair (if you ignore my dye), the same freckles, the same moles in the same places, the same hands, the same voice, the same intonations, and the same date and place of birth: 1 January 1976 in Paris. And a remarkable tendency to think the same thing.

In those seven short hours there isn't a single lull. Our conversation roams in every direction, one thought leading to another, and we both have the same ideas at the same time, or nearly. Several times we burst out laughing because we've embarked on the same sentence, word for word. Perfect stereo. We're two little girls making up for all the time – far too much of it – that we've spent without each other. And it feels so good.

I'm not a specialist in twins but I have some knowledge. We're definitely what's called monozygotic or identical twins, which means we have exactly the same genetic material. Of course, we'd need a DNA test to have full scientific confirmation, but it's so obvious.

The only differences between us relate to our personalities and our lives, which turn out to be such poles apart, and this can't help but have an effect on the way other people see us. We don't use the same vocabulary or wear the same clothes – Juliette is indisputably sexier and more sure of herself – but when it comes to gestures and mannerisms, the likenesses are unmistakable. The way we laugh is absolutely identical, a loud, demonstrative laugh that fits Juliette's personality well and mine much less so, but that's the way I laugh, the same as her. We also have a very distinctive way of frowning with a slight lowering of the head when something annoys us. And lastly, we cry in the same way, punctuating our tears with particularly inelegant sniffing. Hearing these sniffs coming from each other knocks the pain out of the situation, making us burst out laughing halfway through a bout of sobbing.

Lightening the mood to avoid going under. Opening the floodgates without actually drowning, not now, not yet. Thinking things through. Understanding who knew what.

Thirty-nine long years. Fuck.

Juliette talks; she's short of breath and pauses frequently. I hang on her every word, can't take my eyes off her mouth, off her lips as they form her words. I drink in what she's saying and experience her pain when she draws breath. I'm suffocating too, and this mimicry frightens me. Could my hyperventilation actually be a physiological repercussion of my sister's distress, even though I've only just met her? I'm normally so scientific, how can I be drawn in by these ancient beliefs and fantasies about the symmetrical fates of twins? And why not a bit of telepathy while we're at it . . . Still, the peculiar connection in our breathing disturbs me more than I'm prepared to admit.

*

We need a long buffer zone of trivialities before we tackle the most difficult subjects. Oh, OK, so you like Jean-Jacques Goldman too, and broccoli, superhero films, Albert Camus, Niki de Saint Phalle, 'Winter' from Vivaldi's *Four Seasons*, bubble bath, biting into raw pasta, Netflix, lemon meringue pie, the smell of clean sheets, Monica in *Friends*, ping-pong, walnut bread, the number four, mittens, the word 'troglodyte', sleeping on your left side, being woken by the sun, two-flavour bubble gum, George Clooney, and Pringles with guacamole.

It's only after several hours that we decide to tackle our family history. Neither of us wants to go first so we toss a coin: Juliette must start, and I listen as she tells her story, softly and slowly.

'I think . . . I think I have a pretty ordinary life, you

know . . . actually completely ordinary. But completely happy. I've always lived in Avignon, I'm a bit of a homebody. I was only away for a few years and I didn't go very far – I went to uni in Aix-en-Provence but when I found myself there all on my own I felt rootless and wanted to get back to my parents as soon as possible. Typical of an only child, like me. Well, like I *was* until four minutes to ten this morning!'

Juliette tries to smile at me but her smile distorts because it's clear she's never been an only child, we can be sure of that now.

'My parents had trouble conceiving,' she continues. 'My mother told me about it a few years ago, but I got the feeling she still finds it painful to talk about. There weren't all the procedures to help in those days so they had to be patient and just hope that one day maybe . . . When my mother found she was pregnant she was so happy she took lots of photos. I've seen those pictures of her, Romane, of my pregnant mother. She says that when I was born, happiness struck her like a thunderbolt and has never left. I'm not saying that to show off, those are her words – she sometimes has her own way of putting things . . .'

I can't help noticing two things. The first is that Juliette is emphatically listing facts about her parents but carefully avoiding putting them to any sort of test. I'm sure she knows that nothing could be easier than faking a photograph, which means that yellowed old snapshots of her pregnant mother aren't worth much and we're going to need more solid proof. The second thing is that Juliette talks about her mother in the present tense and that gives me a stabbing pain in my chest. Juliette's mother is alive. Is she my mother? My mother may be alive, flippedy flip, my mother may be alive. *Don't say that, Romane, don't think it. Concentrate on Juliette. The rest can come later.*

Juliette can tell I'm feeling emotional. She stares at me intently, hesitating before she goes on. Even though the story of her early life is stirring things up in me, I want to know everything about her. So I smile and my eyes encourage her to keeping going.

'I grew up in a very stable, united family. My parents are still together now. It's amazing, they're in that rare minority of people who still love each other after more than forty-five years together, and they never seem bored. They're faithful in their love and in friendship too . . . they have values, that's what it's called when people are a bit old-school . . . yes, that's it, values. But don't go thinking they're stuck in the mud! They're great people, Romane . . .'

Her discomfort is palpable. In a family like that, you don't lie to your child. It's not part of the blueprint. The next stage of this conversation is going to be painful.

'Romane, I know what you're thinking but I swear to

you, my parents just don't have it in them to lie. They never lie to me, and never have, I'm sure of it, they're my parents. Anyway, everyone's always told me I'm a dead spit of my father. I know where I'm from, my origins are right here in Avignon, with them.'

There's a tremor in her voice as she says this because all these convictions have just been blown apart. I know she's protecting herself, how could I resent her for that? I don't want to railroad her but I can't just sit here in silence.

'Juliette, you know as well as I do that your parents could have covered up a possible adoption; we're going to have to accept that's an option. We're twins, for God's sake! That's the only thing we can be sure of now. Everything else is . . .'

'But I know everything else! They couldn't have . . . it's not possible, Romane. Seriously not possible. I can't believe my parents have been lying to me all these years. And . . . now's really not the time to stir all this up . . .'

She gestures towards her chest and starts to weep silently, breathlessly.

*

I'd like Juliette to tell me about her illness, but first she insists that I talk about my life. I say no, obviously.

'I want to know what's wrong with you, Juliette. We

can't dodge the issue, it's too important. And I'm a doctor, I might be able to help you, you never know.'

'My father's a doctor too, but . . .'

She stops dead.

'But what?'

'But nothing. I'll explain . . . when I've told you what's wrong with me.'

I nod slowly.

'Several weeks ago,' she says, 'I started getting breathless and coughing. I'm naturally optimistic, borderline devil-may-care . . . so at first I thought it must be an allergy, a bad bout of hay fever or some virus that would soon go away. The sort of minor thing that disappears all on its own, with a bit of patience. But then . . . then it got worse. Suddenly. In the last few weeks my cough has got harsher, more intense. I was tired the whole time and felt like I needed to rest twice as much as normal. So I got my act together and went to see the specialists.'

I sit in silence, gripped by fear. I can tell the body blows are only just starting.

'Last week I went to the pulmonology department at the Hôpital Nord to get the results of my tests. I pitched up full of confidence, sure I'd come out with a prescription for antibiotics, maybe need some injections . . . I could see the doctor was beating about the bush, being cautious. I sat there across the desk from him, overplaying my I'm-so-healthy confidence. After a while, given my determination to deny how serious my situation was, he made up his mind to use a word. A terrible word. Just a hypothesis at that stage. But what a hypothesis . . . he used the word cancer, Romane.'

There, that was the uppercut.

I mustn't dissolve, I must be strong, and support her.

I know about lung cancer. A fucking bitch that tens of thousands of people fight every year. And most of them lose. I know the statistics, and they're grim, terrifying. Eighty per cent of sufferers die within five years.

'It's just too much,' Juliette says. 'I mean, I've never smoked a cigarette in my life. The doctors are still running tests, they're not completely sure, and I admit I'm clinging to that uncertainty, but they're very worried. And I can feel it, Romane, I can feel it inside me: whatever it is that's eating away at me is serious . . . I feel like I'm standing by powerless as my body's destroyed one cell at a time. And shockingly quickly.'

Juliette is crying softly. She breaks off from her description. I squeeze her hands, wishing I could reassure her, but I can't help crying too.

'Romane, I have to tell you . . .'

Her solemn voice and the way she pauses make me even more worried.

'My father's a doctor, like I said . . . but he doesn't

know about this. In fact, no one does. I've hidden my illness from my whole family. I've never found the courage to talk to them about it. Cancer's unbearable enough for the person who has it, but for other people . . . I can't, it's impossible. I don't want to cause them pain, I want to protect them, however I can.'

Silence. Coughing. Which goes on too long.

'I've been given so much, Romane, so much love, and happiness . . . and now this bastard illness has put me in this cruel situation . . . making me the one who takes everything away. All the happiness, the light, life itself. How can I agree to play that part? How can I agree to tell my parents and friends I may be dying? And, worse still . . . my own daughter?'

The second uppercut. I falter, sag.

Juliette has a daughter.

She's five and her name is Marie. My own mother's name. A very common name, of course, but its sudden arrival in our conversation is a shock. Yet another. Juliette shows me pictures of her daughter, my niece, and I break down and cry. For a moment, I think I'm looking at a picture of myself as a child.

'Romane, until the prognosis is confirmed, I've decided to fight this in secret, in private. I know some part of Marie would die if I go. That's just how it is, there's nothing anyone can do about it. I think . . . I think no one ever recovers from losing their mother.'

I can't disagree with her. I know. Better than anyone else.

When confronted with illness and death, we all cope as best we can.

Juliette has chosen silence.

It's her choice and I must respect it. Even if I don't agree with it.

My life and problems suddenly feel so meaningless compared to hers. I acknowledge this and I'm furious with myself for my lack of self-control but I can't help it, I need to get out a little bag to breathe into.

I'm definitely not up to this boxing match, completely overwhelmed by the violence in the ring that she's just stepped into.

7

Drowning

Now Juliette's urging me to talk, she wants to know about me too.

As I describe my life, it occurs to me that it might all be a huge fraud. Because Juliette is my twin sister, there's no doubt about that in our minds. One word keeps coming back, weaving its web in the ruins of our neurones. A word we both know we'll never be able to shake off now. So far, Juliette has refused to associate the word with her parents, and I refuse to associate it with my father. But we really will have to grapple with this word that's hovering between us, cutting open our veins and allowing our blood to mingle.

Lie.

Could our lives be delusions? Everything we thought we knew has been swept aside in an instant. Our former lives no longer exist. Juliette and I spend a good hour trying to unravel the threads of our origins. What are the possible scenarios? It feels like an insurmountable task with potentially painful consequences. But we need to understand. To square up to this. We gradually inch the door open and let the darkness in our lives.

Before we go any further, Juliette takes my hand.

'Romane,' she says, 'I . . . I won't have the strength, you need to know this. I won't have the strength to investigate or to talk to my parents. Not now. We'll have to cope without. I'm so sorry . . .'

She starts crying again. I put my arms around her and we sit like that for a while. I stroke her hair and cry with her. I feel I wouldn't resent her, whatever she tells me. We don't have time for that now. Rivalry, squabbling, everything that goes into being a sibling – we've been robbed of all that. I don't know what love between sisters is like but I feel intuitively that it starts with this: being there for her, listening to her, soothing her, boosting her, helping her raise her head high, looking into her eyes and finding in them the strength to go forward.

'I understand, Juliette. Now . . . now there are two of us. I'll help you, as much as I can . . . my sister.'

Why did I add those last two ridiculously abstract words? Perhaps to anchor them in my new reality. Juliette smiles and thanks me. I can see something in her eye now, a subtle spark, a dark corner suddenly lit up. The floodgates are opening and we're agreeing to be submerged. To drown ourselves in the past, together.

It's a difficult conversation at first – it's about our

whole lives, and the protagonists are our parents, so we can't stifle all emotion. We get mired in cloying black mud but we can only see the surface of it; we have no idea what's hiding beneath. So we cry a lot but we make progress, one step at a time.

We don't have a choice. We need to know.

Juliette and I follow four major threads, each of which comprises far too many unacceptable assumptions.

The first is that we're one of those sets of twins deliberately separated at birth by an institution. In this scenario our biological mother would be neither of our two mothers, she would have given birth anonymously and the organization that then took care of us separated us to improve our chances of adoption. Or, worse still, could we have been the subjects of a scientific study? I've heard of stories like this; they seem incredible but they do happen. In theory, twins are perfect material for studying the balance of nature and nurture in an individual's development: what do our genes dictate in how personality evolves, in physical and psychological development? What part is played by our sociocultural environment and our upbringing? What could be better than two individuals who are genetically identical, put into completely different circumstances and then studied for divergences and similarities? Experiments of this sort raise huge ethical questions and are of course illegal. But it's a recognized fact that they did happen in the United States a few decades ago. So why not in France . . . ?

My God, it's all too horrendous.

My father has always been so insistent about how like my mother I am – it's pathological and has proved suffocating, paralysing for me because I felt I wasn't allowed to break away from her. At one stage, my father even went so far as to give me the same hairstyle. I realized this during one of the 'contemplation' sessions he subjected me to as a child: on the first day of every month my father would play my mother's *favourite music*, drink a glass – a bottle – of her *favourite wine*, dress me in her *favourite colour* and do my hair in her *favourite style* (a sort of beehive that I've always loathed and that I changed to a sensible layered cut as soon as I turned fifteen). We would sit and cry over a photo album that I found horribly boring but that broke his heart because, according to him, I was so like her. And I genuinely do look like her. But so many people in the world look alike. Even in films, people find it perfectly credible when two completely unrelated actors play brother and sister. If you want to identify or even emphasize similarities, it's far easier than you think.

In the second scenario, one of our families is the biological family. In that case, which one? And why was one of us abandoned? Taken individually, each of our parents seems sane and incapable of such an abomination.

Yes, but we must now consider every possibility because one thing's for sure: there's nothing normal about any of this.

The third scenario that Juliette and I have come up with – and it's the one we consider the most immoral, if it's even possible to establish a hierarchy of morality in this whole disaster – is child trafficking. Could we have been stolen from our biological mother? Perhaps she was a struggling young woman who had her babies in difficult circumstances, and they were taken from her and offered up for illegal adoptions? Parents longing for a child are prepared to turn a blind eye to plenty of shadowy details about their child's true origins. Or even . . . given that at the time most fathers weren't present at their children's birth, could the theft have taken place without our parents knowing? One of our mothers – but which one? – had twins when she was only expecting a singleton, and the deeply corrupt medical staff took away the second baby . . . Mention of medical staff makes Juliette shudder even more than it does me. Her father's a doctor. He was practising in Paris when Juliette was born. Could he have been implicated in something like this? Juliette doesn't say anything but we've both formulated the possibility in our heads, I'm sure of it.

The fourth and last scenario is the most outlandish but, at the end of the day, one of the least depraved: our real parents are the people we resemble the most. That is, my mother and Juliette's father. Could the two of them have had a relationship, then separated, each taking one of their daughters? How could they have done such a thing? How did our other two parents come into their lives, and when, and why?

Are there other possible scenarios? Most likely. But that's already plenty at this stage. Too much, even. I would never have thought myself capable of imagining such horrors. The whole thing is a nightmare. An utterly bizarre cataclysm that comes hand in hand with bouts of euphoria, I certainly can't deny that: despite how dark these discussions are, Juliette and I are both experiencing a deep-seated happiness because we've found each other at last, when only a few hours ago we didn't know each other existed.

I'm completely lost. I don't know what to think any more.

In any event, one thing is certain.

I need to talk to my father.

As soon as possible.

8

The good old days

At the end of the afternoon Juliette walks to Avignon station with me, and I hop onto the 17.41 high-speed train to Paris. I can't stop taking trains at the moment. For a phobic like me, it smacks of masochism. In the end, though, I'm surprised to find I can lower my guard and let myself be lulled. It has to be said, I've plenty of other things to stress about; the train feels like velvet compared to the mish-mash my life's turning into . . .

*

At bang on nine o'clock the same evening I ring my father's doorbell. I'm not sure I'm up to this, but I need to confront him. I don't have a choice. I've decided to tackle the subject head-on, with no preamble or warning.

I know my father and I know how he reacts to things.

I'll read between the lines and decode his fixed expression.

I'm not sure what I'm expecting. I've naively imagined that when my father discovers what I've found out, he'll break down and admit everything on the spot. Admit what, I don't really know, but there must be something. And if there's nothing to admit, then he'll be shaken to the core. Terrified of the consequences for me, for us both. Empathetic. Protective. A good father.

I tell him about Juliette and show him photos of us together.

He doesn't turn a hair, stays calm, makes fun of the whole business.

'My princess, I do wonder where you get your ideas from . . . you've always had quite an imagination, but this . . . Are you feeling all right? I worry about you, you know . . . about your health . . . I think you've lost weight since you left home . . . maybe you should come and see me more . . .'

I know my father by heart. I can see the discomfort in his evasive eyes and the slight quiver in his upper lip despite the fake assurance he's putting on.

This sidestepping response isn't right; it's *not normal.*

And I'm immediately convinced my father's lying to me.

The conversation grinds to a halt. I sit down on the sofa in the living room, crestfallen, and the tears start to flow. I've lost all control.

He, on the other hand, is completely in control. He's been in control for thirty-nine years. I should have guessed he wouldn't cave. He comes over and puts a hand on my hunched back.

'Don't cry, darling, please. It upsets me to see you like this . . . You should stay here, with me. I'll take care of you, like in the good old days.'

This expression, combined with his composure and his smile (innocent as a child taking first Communion), does something to me; I can feel hysteria rising inside me. I jump to my feet and turn nasty.

'There never were any good old days, Dad. The good old days don't exist. All there's been is lies and fakery, from the start. You're lying, Dad! I don't know what it is you're ashamed of but you're lying!'

'I won't have you talking to me like that, Romane. I'm your father, and that's an end to it. I don't know what's put these ideas in your head but I swear on your mother's grave that I *am* your father, in God's name!'

Then he gives me that old refrain, 'How could you? After everything I've done for you.' But I've already stopped listening. I've moved on.

What's he hiding from me?

He asks me to give him a few minutes. He'll show me, seeing as it's come to this. He reappears – peculiarly quickly, it seems to me. As if this proof has been waiting a long time, ready to leap to his help. As if he's been anticipating this onslaught for a long time. I can see he won't move an inch. He hands me some papers: a birth certificate and a medical report about my mother, saying she had a normal pregnancy. It all looks authentic but how would I know? It's so easy to falsify documents, and he was far too quick. If someone asked me to find last year's tax return, it would take me more than five minutes . . . so a hospital report from 1976 . . .

I'm sure it's all fake.

'You're lying, Dad! You want to know how I dare talk to you like this? The question is how can you look me in the eye? How dare *you*? I come here to tell you I've got a twin sister and you behave as if I'm losing my mind. Tell me the truth! Do you think Mum would be happy to see us like this? Do you think she'd be proud of you?'

I stop dead and hold my breath because I've suddenly seen something in my father's eyes that I've never seen before. A sort of violence.

It's at this point that I lose control and he takes it back. Or vice versa, I'm not sure. My father slaps me.

It's the first time in my life that he's raised a hand to me. Hmm. I thought I knew my father but I now realize I know nothing about him or the man he once was. He's never told me anything about his life *before me*, apart from his time with my mother, which is bound to have been embellished by the power of memory – or lies.

And this fact hits me in the face, literally. I bring my hand to my cheek and sit motionless, reeling.

A stealthy anger starts to chafe inside me, mingled with sadness and fear. My brain's working at full capacity. Some parts of my father's narrative must be false. Which, I don't know. But he doesn't seem keen to cooperate.

I make my way to the bathroom and he follows me. I lock myself in, still sniffing, and splash myself with water, bellowing at him through the door to leave me alone. From out in the corridor he apologizes. Again and again. He doesn't know what came over him, he can't forgive himself for slapping me. Then he starts crying too . . . but still sticks to his version of the facts: he's my father. And he loves me.

'This girl does look like you, I can't deny it. But there are seven billion people on the planet . . . seven billion, Romane! There are bound to be likenesses in this old world. You're unique, my one and only daughter, my beloved daughter. I love you, Romane, I love you so much. I'm here if you need to talk. I'll always be here for you, my princess.'

While he's talking, I pluck some hairs from his ancient hairbrush. Some of them still have their roots attached. Perfect. I must get this right, though, so I need another sample. I find a pair of nail clippers and use it to cut a few bristles from his toothbrush. This meticulous but undetectable process of harvesting evidence is worthy of a bad episode of *CSI*, I think to myself incongruously in this moment of quiet.

I race out of the bathroom and slip out of the apartment, ignoring my father's shouts and calls and, later, his texts.

*

I nip home and throw together a suitcase in record time – ten little minutes, I've never been so speedy – because I've decided to spend the night in a hotel next to Gare de Lyon to avoid suffering my father's intrusion into my home. I know he has a set of my keys and I have absolutely no desire to listen to him trying to persuade me his lies are true.

Deep down inside me, there's still a little voice protesting that he might be telling the truth, that he never knew Juliette existed and he really is my father. Is that possible? His behaviour this evening proves otherwise, or at least suggests something different because he seemed so prepared and it all sounded so wrong. If he hadn't known anything, he would – like me – have tried to understand . . . rather than producing documents like a rabbit out of a hat.

In the middle of the night and in just a few clicks – the Internet's a godsend! – I identify several companies in Spain, Belgium and the US that offer a quick, reliable and good-quality service. I opt for the swiftest, Belgium, and first thing in the morning I post off an envelope with hair and toothbrush bristles from Juliette, my father and myself. Ideally, I would also have included samples from Juliette's parents but she couldn't get her hands on anything straight away and I don't want to waste any time. I need to know. I'll get the results online in four to six days.

If my father won't talk, his DNA can do it for him.

9

The pact

I think I loved Juliette from the very first moment.

They call it love at first sight and I've never felt it for anyone. In my defence, I've never been confronted with a twin sister before . . .

So I haven't put up a fight, I've accepted this devastatingly instant, inexplicable, animal-like love. I feel that every second counts now so I can't afford the luxury of not loving her straight away, unconditionally. And she feels the same way about me; I felt it and she told me and I believe her. We've established a completely natural, inevitable bond of trust.

Just before I left Avignon for Paris yesterday Juliette asked me something.

Much more than a favour.

'You know, Romane,' she said, 'I think our meeting like this, today, at this point in my life . . . it's a sign, it's meant to be.'

'You mean . . . like some inexplicable force from the

furthest reaches of the universe?' I asked solemnly, then gave her a huge smile.

'Don't laugh at me,' she protested, rolling her eyes. 'I'm not mad!'

'I'm not laughing, Juliette, I'm smiling . . . because I don't believe all that mumbo jumbo about signs sent by cosmic entities . . . and anyway, they could have sent their flipping signs a bit sooner, don't you think?'

'Whether you like it or not, you've turned up in my life exactly when I need a miracle.'

'I'm not sure I understand . . .'

'*You're* the miracle, Romane! There, you weren't expecting that, were you? No one's ever said that to you, have they?'

She laughed . . . and I could feel the reverberations of her laugh in me. She was right, there's something supernatural about it all.

'I need you, Romane,' she said. 'I mean it. I need you and I know you'll help me. You've come at just the perfect time, or maybe it's the worst time, it doesn't matter. You've come into my life through a hidden door . . . and it's changed my whole outlook.'

'Please, Juliette, tell me what you're thinking . . .'

'Thanks to you, Romane, I can carry on hiding the fact that I'm ill. You can help me keep my secret. And spare my daughter. And maybe – who knows – keep doing that forever.'

A big red light went on in my head and I physically took a step back. She couldn't help noticing.

'I know, it sounds crazy when I say it like that, and it is . . . Are you happy in your life, Romane? I got the feeling . . . I don't know, I got the feeling that–'

'That I'm not happy. You're right, I'm not. My life was already full of gaping holes and in the last few hours they've become cavernous abysses.'

'I love the way you talk, Romane . . . so chic. Sorry, I know this isn't a good time to tease you.'

She laughed again, then coughed, for a long time. I wished I could get my hands on it right that minute, this cosmic entity that's choking her.

By the time Juliette started talking again, I was already shaking because I knew. I knew why she was sidestepping the issue, making jokes and losing herself in rhetorical convolutions.

'My life's wonderful, Romane,' she said eventually. 'It's full of pleasures and laughter and happiness. I don't want to ruin all that, I don't want to destroy the people I love. They don't deserve it.'

Juliette clasped my right hand between her hands, as if to ensure I couldn't run away after hearing what she was about to say.

'That's where you come in, Romane. I know what you're going to say so please let me speak, and then think about it. Don't react straight away. OK?'

'OK.'

'Promise?'

'I promise,' I said, then I added earnestly, 'You have my solemn promise.'

A pause. An eternity.

'Romane . . . this pact I'm suggesting is . . . a crazy idea and it'll be difficult to carry out. Impossible, in theory. Except that in the last few hours we've both realized that nothing's impossible. Romane . . . I want you to take my place in my life if I'm going to die. To spare my family and friends . . . and my daughter – your niece – the agony of grief. It's wrong to die at my age. No one expects it. It would be such a shock . . . I want everything to carry on as normal, as it is now. I'm sure you'd be happy in my life, Romane.'

I took it on board, said nothing, looked away. Juliette is so devoted to these people, she talks about them with such love and passion that it's terrifying. I don't think I've ever felt such a visceral need to ensure another person's happiness. Not even my father's. Which of us is more unhinged? I wondered. Either way, Juliette is more alive.

'Juliette, there's no way. You can't *seriously* be contemplating me taking your place . . . can you?'

She nodded silently.

'Well, then it's no. No, no and no. I think the shock of hearing how ill you are has made you lose your grip on reality. You're going to live, for heaven's sake! I'm here and I'll support you, but you can't ask me to do the unthinkable.'

'I knew that's what you'd say, it's only natural. I wasn't expecting you to jump for joy and say, "Yay, of course, off you go and die and let me get stuck in here." In fact, your reaction's pretty reassuring, but promise me you'll think about it, Romane.'

'I've already said I will.'

'Do I have your solemn promise?' she asked with a hint of a smile.

'You have my solemn promise.'

'In the meantime . . . I have a *huge* favour to ask.'

'I can't see how any favour could be more *huge* than what we've just been talking about.'

'OK, so I used the word "huge" deliberately so this favour would seem much more doable. And so you'd say yes straight away. It's a sales technique: you say something's going to be very expensive and then when you name the price – which isn't all that bad – the buyer's relieved and buys the thing on the spot. I know they don't teach you that at medical school . . .'

Her smile. Her gentle mockery. I melted, which was the intended effect.

'I'm all ears.'

'I want . . . what I'd like, please, would be for you . . . for you to take my place for a few days. Just this week. I don't want to put my family into a panic for no reason until the diagnosis is there in black and white. I have to go back to Marseilles on Tuesday for more tests. To find out once and for all what's happening to my body. I beg you, Romane. Help me.'

I refused again, but promised I'd think about it.

And that's what I'm doing tonight in my hotel by Gare de Lyon station.

Crazy as it may seem, a cry for help like that can't be taken lightly. I can't ignore such distress coming from a sister I didn't know existed but who's so irresistibly endearing. So I'm lying here considering her proposal. Not just the one about the few days, but the other one too, the definitive one.

Am I losing my mind?

Would it really be a big loss to change my life? What's kept me alive so far is my father's happiness. It's taken a massive electric shock to make me realize that living alone with your father isn't really a life.

Saying yes to Juliette would mean giving up on my own life.

Turning my back on my work wouldn't be all that hard. I like tending to people but I'm not the hard-bitten type who can't contemplate anything outside medicine. After all, a few happy finds in a bookshop can sometimes do as much good as a medicinal tonic.

Giving up my friends wouldn't be difficult either. As

I formulate this idea, I realize how terribly sad it is. Apart from my friend Melissa – and perhaps I could stay in touch with her? – there's no one I'd really miss.

No one except my father. The hardest thing would be never seeing him again. After what's just happened, breaking away from him might seem more manageable, and I'm no longer even sure he's my biological father, but whatever he's done, he'll always be my dad. I'll always love him. If I ever agree to this no-way-back pact with Juliette, I just wouldn't give him a choice: I would explain and he'd have to accept it, end of story.

As my thoughts evolve, I can see that Juliette's outlandish idea is starting to take shape, to become a reality. The conditional is morphing into the future tense . . . as if I'm already agreeing to take on my sister's life more wholeheartedly than I ever have my own.

Get a grip, Romane. I mean, flippedy flip, what the hell are you thinking?

I shake my head to drive away the disturbing absurdity of it. Taking Juliette's place for the rest of my life isn't on the agenda. It never will be. I *can* help her, though. After my painful confrontation with my father, I now feel Juliette is the only family I can really trust. And standing in for her for a few days is really very little to ask.

So I decide to accept. To play the part, just for a week.

I accept so that she can go back to Marseilles for more

tests without arousing the suspicions of her loved ones. I'll try to protect her silence and give her some time. I'll undertake to do this but I'll make one thing very clear: I can't give any guarantees. After all, we're talking about passing myself off as her with the people who know her best . . .

The whole situation is so surreal.

After these few days we'll both go back to normal and Juliette will have to find the strength to talk to her family. She'll tell them and I'll support her. I won't abandon her. It's clear to me that, whatever we find out about our origins, Juliette will always see her parents as her parents. Right now, she has better things to worry about than calling into question a family she loves and that loves her.

At 6.07 on Monday, 20 July 2015, I get onto another train bound for Avignon.

As soon as I'm sitting in my seat I say yes to Juliette, sealing our fates with just a text. And I receive the heartbreakingly simple reply: *Thank you.*

As I read those two little words, I feel terror bubbling up inside me and urgently reach for a paper bag.

Flippedy-dippedy-flip-flip. What have I done? It's total madness. It won't last a single day. It's too enormous, too unthinkable. But I've just agreed to it. I could pretend to wonder why, but the answer's clear as day: because I desperately want to.

Obviously, the main reason I've agreed is to help my sister . . . but I can't lie, it's not the only reason.

The truth is, I have this furious urge to meet Juliette's parents. I need to see them with my own eyes. I want to get to know them because they may be my parents. Ever since yesterday, a little voice deep inside me has been clamouring, trying to tell me that my biological mother may be alive, she may be Juliette's mother. It's such an emotional upheaval. So revolutionary. I bite my lip, hard, punishing myself for what I see as disloyalty to my father. To think how much he's done for me, and he so eloquently reminded me of that yesterday. To think how much I love him, from the depths of my soul. But let's be sensible about this: pursuing the truth doesn't mean denying love. I know in advance I'd never be able to hate him, whatever he may have done. But if I also have a living mother . . .

Just before I left Avignon late on Sunday afternoon, Juliette put a sign on her shop door saying it would stay closed until Monday evening. She was sure I'd say yes.

Monday. That's today. Just one day. We're going to need every minute of it to transform me into Juliette. I need to learn to be her. Learn about the bookshop and her day-to-day life. Learn how she moves and her favourite expressions, learn to be like her and to imitate her. Or at least to create the illusion.

Breathe, Romane, it'll all be fine. Have faith in yourself, for once. If you can't have faith in yourself, then have faith in Juliette. She's convinced you can do it, so why aren't you?

I can't wait. I'm frightened. I'm excited. I'm terrified.

To my very core I can feel just how right my decision is. Perhaps I'm being reckless, but for the first time in ages, it feels as if I'm doing something good. That I matter to someone other than my father.

And I think it's making me happy.

Despite the thoughts that have me in such a jitter, despite feeling overwhelmed as the train carries me back to Avignon, I fall into a strange sleep.

As deep as the lake I've just thrown myself into. With my eyes wide open.

THAT DAY

It was 1 January 1976, around daybreak. I woke with a start, sweating and breathless. I couldn't remember anything about the dream that had put me in this unpleasant clammy state, but my stomach was tied in knots. An incongruous conviction had settled in the pit of my abdomen: something strange was going to happen that day. I saw that my radio alarm wasn't working and checked my watch: 6.38. The alarm usually went off twelve minutes later. Waking early spontaneously had left me with an acrid taste in my mouth. A taste of something unfinished that I'd never shake off. Bloody power cuts. This was the middle of Paris and thousands of households had been without electricity or phone lines for several days.

I got out of bed, wound up the shutter and stood there for a moment watching the to and fro of refuse collectors. The sky was laden and the city was cloaked in mist as dense as the snow that covered everything. Christmas and New Year usually launch the city headlong into a frothy spree of consumerism but that year was different. The velvety air muffled sounds and dampened the exuberance. Hampered the traffic. Paris wasn't equipped for such bad weather, it didn't know how to deal with it. The city was slumbering. Further power failures were expected for the 1st, a bank holiday. We'd just have to sit it out; engineers were doing what they could but the fresh snowfall of the last few hours wasn't helping. Still, the teams at EDF and France Télécom wanted to wish everyone in Paris a happy new year.

I really didn't feel like going out. And certainly not to work. What with alcoholic comas, cold-water drownings, road traffic accidents and the other consequences of risk-taking New Year's Eve behaviour, I knew it would be a hard day at the hospital. What I didn't know was that it would be much harder in the outside world.

Your mother was still asleep. I could hear her regular breathing as it raised the thick covers. New Year's Eve had felt strange that year: we'd spent it at home, just the two of us. Which suited us perfectly. I was on duty on New Year's Day. I couldn't get the day off and she'd known that so she'd decided we should spend the last evening of our last year as just a couple . . . as just a couple. We hadn't realized at the time that we'd have to make do with a rudimentary meal, the two of us wrapped in blankets to ward off the biting cold seeping into the apartment.

In the end, our candlelit evening was magical. We spent it snuggled together, discussing all the happiness to come.

'In less than five weeks there'll be three of us. She'll be right here beside us. Can you believe it? Will she be healthy? Who will she look like? What shape will her nose be? What colour eyes will she have?'

It might be difficult to believe now, but we hadn't seen you yet. Forty years ago scans were a luxury; fewer than 10 per cent of women had them in 1975, and they were usually carried out in the first weeks, to date the pregnancy accurately. We were lucky to be part of that minority. A test image was taken during the first trimester, but it was difficult to interpret, even for me as a doctor. Obviously, it was impossible to make out the baby's sex, but your mother was convinced you were a girl. So convinced that she only ever referred to you as 'she'. Every now and then I reminded her that we couldn't be sure of anything, but I'd got used to the idea too. Imagining my daughter made it easier for me to see myself in the role of father – an idealized role that was worlds away from the reality I would actually experience, but it was still intense and vivid. Your birth was becoming an inescapable fact. You were becoming real for me, and I could only feel you kicking through the filter of your mother's distended tummy.

It was cold in the apartment that morning; the temperature had dropped further overnight. I got ready as quietly as possible, by torchlight. I picked up the handset of the phone: the line was still dead. As expected. I left a little note for your mother, saying how much I loved you, both of you, my two sleeping princesses. I closed the door and hauled on my coat as I hurried down the crooked old staircase. The building was deserted. We'd joked about this three days earlier with the concierge, and even she was away today, which was very unusual: on the first day of 1976, in a building that comprised twelve apartments, ours was the only one occupied. The concierge had entrusted the keys to her rooms to your mother, who'd promised to keep an eye on comings and goings and any suspect behaviour – 'you never know what people might get up to on a bank holiday, the things you see nowadays!' I tied my scarf in the hallway, preparing to confront the bitter winter air, the strong wind and my job as a junior doctor in A & E at Hôtel-Dieu Hospital.

*

The day wore on, exhaustingly. I kept breaks to the absolute minimum, a few cups of coffee knocked back hastily, a so-called festive lunch ploughed through in less than ten minutes. The occasional Father Christmas hat trying to cheer the place up didn't fool anyone: patients and staff alike, everyone would rather have been somewhere else. We all put a brave face on it, trying our best to smile.

Every time I could steal a moment from the constant buzz of A & E, I went to the admissions desk and dialled the number for our apartment – the hospital had miraculously been spared in the power failures. Engaged. Which meant the line was still down. I missed your mother. When I was on duty on Christmas Day she'd called me every hour. It became a game with the receptionists who passed on her messages and congratulated me for having such a loving wife. I was proud. I've always been proud of your mother. I still am now. She knew what I was like, she knew I couldn't help my imagination going off down tortuous rabbit holes when I left her on her own. So ever since we'd known she was pregnant, she would call me regularly when I was on duty. To stop me fretting.

I'd agreed to be on duty for all the public holidays that year, hoping my turn would come the next year and we could make the most of our first Christmas as a threesome. As a family. My little family.

*

Before leaving the hospital I tried to call her one last time – still with no success. In the absence of a telephone line, I hoped at least the heating would be back on in the apartment. When I stepped out into the street at about seven o'clock in the evening it was cold and dark. A cloudy, starless January night. I hurried because it was starting to snow again. I pictured her curled up in our bed reading, and the image reassured me but I could feel the muscles in my back stiffening as I drew closer to home. Probably a combined effect of sub-zero temperatures and my unfounded fears.

I went into our building and smiled briefly because the electricity was working again. I started to climb the stairs, cursing the seven floors I had to tackle. We'd discussed moving house: we knew those stairs would be tricky once we had you. In fact, your mother had already been cutting down on outings for several weeks. She'd put on weight rapidly through December and it took her a long time to drag herself all the way up to our apartment.

When I reached the fourth floor, already out of breath, I swore I'd start looking for a new apartment the very next day.

When I reached the fifth floor I paused and pulled off my scarf. The temperature had risen in the common parts . . . I pictured running myself a hot bath, and quickened my pace.

When I reached the sixth floor my eye was drawn to a dark patch on the floor. I knelt to look at it more closely. Put my finger to it. I started to shake, looked up and felt my heartrate quicken. It wasn't the only patch. There were others, longer ones, trails. On the sixth-floor landing. On the stairs to the next floor.

When I reached the seventh floor my pulse accelerated. I felt a wave of panic welling inside me. Our door was ajar. The trail of blood was more or less continuous. My guts churned, paralysing my mind. I tore into the apartment, bellowing your mother's name, amazed to find myself noticing that the lights were on. As if that mattered.

She wasn't in the living room.

My eyes clouded when I heard a cry that felt like an echo of my own terror. A baby's cry. I pulled myself together, took a deep breath and called your mother once, twice, three times. I made my way down the corridor, hastily piecing together the most likely scenario: she'd had the baby. On her own. It all happened too quickly. She was cut off from the world, with no phone. She'd tried to get out, went down one floor, then retraced her steps. There was too much pain, she was frightened by the blood loss. She'd had the courage and the strength to climb back up. I admired her, I loved her, she'd coped like a champion, she'd gone through hell and there was the result: I could hear my baby crying.

But why couldn't I hear her?

I went into the bedroom. She was lying on the bed. You were nestled in the crook of her arm. She'd cut your cord and kept you close to her. She was right all along, you were a girl. I wept. You were so beautiful. Your mother was facing away from me. She didn't speak, didn't respond. She didn't answer, whatever I said.

I walked around the bed and the floor gave way beneath my feet. Her lips were blue. Her body was cold. I shook her, shouted louder. The truth hit me as the sobs rose up in my chest. She had no right to do this to me, not today, not like this, never. I put my fingers to her neck but I already knew. I tried heart massage but it didn't change anything. I howled her name till I felt my chest might split open. I took you in my arms and collapsed on the floor. I held you tightly to me, against my beating heart, and my body shook uncontrollably. It just wasn't possible. It wasn't possible. Why hadn't I come home earlier? Why had I agreed to work that day? If I'd been there, she'd have been there too. With me. With you.

I gave a great guttural, instinctive wail. A lament from the very depths.

My love.

I kept you hugged tightly to me and all at once I heard her. I thought I recognized your mother's laugh, but that wasn't what it was. I looked down at you and stopped crying, silenced by the surprise. The terror.

I stood up. Slowly.

And that's when I saw her.

Her limbs flailing in a pool of blood as dark as what she'd just done.

Unexpected. Diabolical. Iniquitous. Murderous.

My second daughter.

PART 2

Days

10

Monday

New look, new life

Juliette's waiting for me in the station car park, standing next to her pink Twingo – I loathe pink, which is awkward. Yesterday when I told her I couldn't drive she gave me a gentle ribbing.

'I honestly wonder how you've survived this long . . . but you do have running water, don't you, in that little capital city of yours?'

She's right, not having a driving licence is pretty exceptional for someone my age. But I find Parisian public transport less frightening than driving myself. I've never taken the plunge and it's never been a problem for me, not at all.

The closer I get to the car, the more beautiful Juliette looks. Somehow both natural and sophisticated. Just a little make-up, her hair scooped up and held in place with a simple clip. She's luminous, dazzling, but in such an understated way in her pairing of a fluid blouse and denim shorts with woven leather sandals. In startling contrast with my look: brown 'bed-head' hair (which actually means I haven't brushed it), shapeless blue T-shirt and boring skirt. It's going to take some work to haul me up to her level. My mind alights on an old-fashioned expression to say to her and I can't think of another. Never mind . . .

'You're all bright-eyed and bushy-tailed!'

'Thanks . . . Grandma!' she says with a big smile, and when I pretend to be upset, 'I'm teasing you, I love your anachronistic expressions. You'll just have to leave them out for a few days.'

I scour my brain to come up with an inspired reply to make her eyes twinkle like that again.

'No problemo, I can do my best street talk, innit, blood?'

Juliette bursts out laughing but then stops abruptly and turns away so that I don't see her cough . . . It goes on for some time but she's still laughing too.

'OK, Romane, you're getting more up-to-date with your vocab but you want to watch where you go with it . . . we've only got a day to get this right, you know!'

I ask if she's feeling well enough to drive and she says glibly of course she is, she's not dead yet. I get the feeling she could brighten any difficult situation. I can sense a strength in her, a lust for life that could move mountains.

As she drives she explains the agenda for the day. A

very busy agenda. She will slip away first thing tomorrow morning because her appointment is at 9.30.

She tells me that her daughter won't actually be around all week. She was meant to be picking her up today but has managed to convince Raphaël, her ex-partner, to switch weeks. Without disclosing anything to him, of course. Juliette and Raphaël didn't marry, Juliette is 'against marriage, solemn undertakings and all that shit', but they're still on very good terms. She still loves him in some ways. It's different, obviously, but he's the father of her daughter so there'll always be a strong connection.

'Marie's staying with Raphaël until next Monday. It'll be easier for you, you'll have plenty to deal with as it is, without being lumbered with my princess.'

Juliette thinks she's done the right thing and her intentions are admirable. I don't say anything, managing to control my emotions, but I'm terribly disappointed. For years now I've felt what many people feel if they're still single at my age, something that weighs even more heavily than loneliness: the absence of children. I loved the thought of pretending to be my sister and looking after my niece for a few days. But Juliette's right, this will be easier.

For a while we meander through spectacular scenery dotted with Provençal vineyards. The light is blinding, almost black. I screw up my eyes and can already make out the village of Châteauneuf-du-Pape up on the hillside. It's dominated by an old keep that Juliette tells me is a vestige of the former papal residence built in the fourteenth century. She parks the car in a narrow medieval street shaded by thick stone walls. We sit on a solid wooden beam set into a block of rock and Juliette takes two bottles of water from her handbag – what she calls a 'designer it-bag' . . . what I call a simple canvas tote decorated with silver sequins. We both drink, tipping our heads back and looking up at the sky. A final lull before the tumult of the days to come. An oasis of calm in all the seething upheaval. A moment of quiet contemplation.

Juliette turns to me. She looks happy, at peace.

'We're half an hour from where I live but I must have only been here twice in my life. I thought it was the perfect place for a bit of a makeover in peace and quiet. I know too many people in Avignon, the whole plan would fall apart if one of my neighbours saw us together. And anyway, we can then find a good restaurant afterwards . . . and great wine!'

'Hmm . . . are you sure you want to drink? I don't know if that's a good idea . . . and you'll be driving afterwards . . .'

She's giving me the jitters with her suggestion. My hand automatically darts into my bag, trying to find my paper allies. She can't help noticing.

'It's OK, Romane, don't stress. Come on, I can have a small glass of wine, can't I? It won't kill me, will it? I won't drive us into a ditch . . . put your sick bags away, everything's fine, the situation's under control. Come on, let's go!'

She holds out her hand to me, as if inviting me to dance. I put my hand in hers, do a modest balletic leap and we head towards Last Tangle in Paris (with me hoping they're better at their job than they are at puns). We go in and Juliette explains with great simplicity that I need to come out looking exactly like her.

'We were so alike when we were little, we want to be like that again. You know, we're so close . . .'

The hairdresser – sporting an improbable Gothic look – is thrilled with the challenge and takes it very seriously. Colour, cut and make-up. I get the whole shebang with plenty of patient advice. It has to be said that mascara, eyeliner and foundation are all rather exotic for me; I've only worn them three or four times in my life.

Two hours later I'm a different woman.

I'm her.

Once the transformation is complete and I see myself in the mirror, I can't hold back my tears.

My thoughts are in turmoil: this isn't me, it's Juliette I'm seeing. In a few days I'll be Romane again and all this will be over, melting away along with the pumpkin carriage.

It's strange because I'm also thinking the exact opposite: maybe today is a fresh start for me, it's up to me alone to stay as this woman now, and I too have a right to feel beautiful. Because I do feel beautiful as I sit here, looking into this mirror in a hair salon. It's an unbearably powerful moment for someone like me who's only ever had a very low opinion of her physical appearance. My clothes suddenly feel completely wrong, I want to throw them away, to burn them.

'That's the next stage, we'll get to that,' Juliette says, laughing.

I'm still crying softly, and the hairdresser curses because it's taken me just moments to destroy all her hard work with the make-up. Juliette and I can't help laughing like idiots, though. Eventually my makeover artist – who proved very talented – swallows her irritation and laughs along with us.

Over lunch Juliette goes through instructions about the bookshop and her apartment. Before I'd even said yes, she used the time when I went back up to Paris to draft and print out a document with all the key information. She will add to it as the day goes on, while we talk things through. Access codes; opening hours; which key for which door; phone numbers for her mother, her father, Raphaël, her best friend Corinne ('she's on holiday in Brittany, she shouldn't call or come to see you this week'); a simplified family tree with anecdotes about each person; certain things to say to her mother and father 'to be more realistic' . . . these pages are a survival kit and it immediately feels indispensable, but it also piles on the pressure.

I'm gradually realizing the enormity of the task I've set myself. Juliette can see what I'm thinking and manages to calm me. To play things down.

'It'll only be a few minutes with each of them. Raphaël and Marie have gone to his parents' near Nice. You're bound to see my mother, though. She drops in at the shop at least three times a week. She might ask you over for supper but you can say no, say you've got other plans or you're tired . . . I'm not sure you'll see my father. He thinks it's far too hot to go out at the moment, so he's staying at home. They've got a nice house with air conditioning and a swimming pool on the outskirts of Avignon, it's his haven of peace, so if he *can* avoid walking around among drunken festival-goers, that suits him fine.'

Juliette pauses, takes a moment to catch her breath. She smiles at me.

I smile back and am careful not to shout out loud how desperately I want to meet her parents. Juliette has stopped talking about where we came from; she doesn't seem to be haunted by the need to know, the feverish longing that I can't shake off. Despite how important this question is, Juliette has blotted it out. Would it drop into the background for me too, if I were in her shoes? Of course it would. She's probably right: she needs to focus her energies on the hardest, most immediate battle. What would be the point of calling her whole life into question just when she's preparing to confront death? When a ship is adrift, everyone needs to choose a course, to have a working compass, if they're to resist succumbing to panic and uncertainty.

'Everything'll be fine, Romane. OK, so I do have a lot of customers at the shop and a lot of acquaintances in Avignon, but you can just pretend, say hello, give them a big open smile and you'll be fine. If they start a conversation, let them talk first and you'll soon get a feel for how well they know you . . .'

Another pause. Another painful cough. Another smile.

'And we're all hyperconnected these days: if we're too busy, we can always fall back on the good old phone call that has to be answered or the meeting that can't be missed, they always work. And if someone points out something you've forgotten, make a joke of it. It happens. We're all allowed to make mistakes, aren't we?'

She's probably right. I'm making too much of this, as usual. I need to calm down.

*

Once back in Avignon, we're careful not to go to Juliette's apartment together. She drops me off near the old ramparts and I do the last part on foot, guided by my phone. There are still just as many people on the streets but it doesn't feel quite so hot today. Or am I getting used to it? I haven't had a chance to check the weather, I don't know if the heatwave is cooling but I'm finding it easier to breathe.

I spend part of the afternoon learning to dress like Juliette, then I study photographs, getting to know the faces of the people who will be part of my world in a few hours' time. Juliette asks to see a photo of my father, something she didn't have the courage to ask yesterday. I don't have one and I didn't even think of it. My father has always had a phobia of being photographed, and the arrival of smartphones hasn't made things any easier for him. Like me, he thinks it's dangerous leaving images of yourself on a device that can so easily be stolen or hacked. Anyone could get their hands on it, MI5, hackers, pickpockets . . . Neither of us wants to find our faces associated with a crime scene or a false passport so we don't take photos. Ever. In fact, the ones Juliette and I took of us together yesterday are the only photos on my phone. Juliette laughs and says we really are a couple of paranoids. She's right there.

Next I work on adopting Juliette's habits and tics. She bites her nails, nibbles the ends of biros, twists her hair around a finger when she talks, and punctuates her sentences with 'obviously' and 'd'you see what I mean?' . . . I'll try to imitate that.

Then she tells me about the bookshop. I warn her I'm not very literary and I won't know what advice to give to customers.

'Not everyone's looking for advice, you know, particularly at this time of year. Some come for a specific book, others just want to browse in an air-conditioned space for a few minutes. Don't worry if you don't know what to say, you can't know everything. Mind you, I warn you, you're likely to hear some absolute gems . . .'

'Some what?'

'Some gems . . . people who ask if you've got a copy of Beckett's *Waiting for Lotto* or *Wuthering Heists* or even Rambo's poems . . .'

'You're definitely exaggerating,' I chuckle. 'That sort of thing can't happen very often, surely?'

'More often than you'd think . . . promise you'll text me if someone asks for Homer's *Oddity* or Dickens's *Our Mutual Fiend*!'

I'm crying with laughter but I manage to promise. My solemn promise!

Next Juliette talks me through procedures for the job. There shouldn't be anything too ambitious to do this week, all the big orders are in and she has plenty of stock.

'But there's always someone who needs a book you

don't have, so you'll need to know how to handle orders. And the till, obviously.'

I'm not great at anything to do with computers so what might have taken half an hour with someone else takes us a good hour. She doesn't complain, just explains tirelessly, still smiling. She stops to cough, gets her breath back and then sets off again. It hurts me to watch her. The more time I spend with her, the more I think this illness has no right to threaten her like this. She deserves to live. My heart constricts with every spasm in her lungs.

I spend a wonderful evening with her and we don't get much sleep, but do eventually fall asleep together in her double bed – two thirty-nine-year-old little girls who may look a bit ridiculous holding hands all through the night but they don't want to spend a single second apart.

*

When Tuesday comes, I can't say I'm completely relaxed about this.

But I'm ready.

At 7.30 Juliette gives me a big hug.

I take her phone and give her mine. Phones are probably the most personal thing anyone has these days, they contain everything. Swapping phones amounts to swapping lives. Which is exactly what we're doing.

Juliette's eyes are clouded with tears as she says goodbye. The taxi's waiting, she needs to go and I can't follow her out, someone might see us. As she lets go of my hand with a last smile, I see a terrible wave of sadness in her eyes. I close the door and the same wave washes over me. I have the peculiar feeling that I've just hugged my sister for the last time. I try to dispel this dark thought but it clings cruelly to my mind.

Still, I can't stand here feeling sorry for myself. I don't have time.

I've got a hairstyle and a make-up routine to reproduce – and God knows, I'm not used to that – and a bookshop to open. I've got a whole day of lies to live.

I take a deep breath and get on with this ridiculous promise I've made. Despite the powerful emotions at work on me, a strange feeling of joy gradually suffuses me as I transform myself into Juliette. It's something close to happiness.

Because I'm helping my sister.

Because deep down I'm convinced she's going to pull through this.

Because I can see that knowing I'm here watching her back makes her calmer, gives her more strength and spirit to battle her illness.

Because I know that what I'm doing isn't only for her. I agreed to do this for me too. It's for me first and foremost.

I'm shaky, nervous, excited, anxious.

I put the finishing touches to my lipstick and smile at this new face in the mirror. She doesn't look that bad after all.

Everything about her looks furiously alive.

11

Tuesday

Firsts

I open the bookshop at the agreed time and arrange the vases of white flowers just inside the door – with this heat, Juliette said, I shouldn't put them out on the pavement because they would probably die within a few hours. I definitely don't have green fingers so I admit that without this advice from my sister I would probably have killed them on the very first day.

I like the bookshop, it has a welcoming atmosphere. Juliette has arranged it into several clearly defined spaces: a large, polished wood table, with impressive pyramids of books and 'favourite read' cards on various fiction titles; a low pedestal table next to two brown leather chairs for leafing through something from the range of coffee-table books; and an apple-green beanbag, soft lighting, a vintage school desk and felt tips in a pot shaped like a London taxi for the children's area. Juliette explained that her bookshop is her home and she spends more time here than in her apartment upstairs, so she might as well feel comfortable, and she likes her guests – her customers – to enjoy their time in the shop too.

I'm not a great reader but I've always loved bookshops. And I love that special smell books have. At my father's house – I nearly said 'at home', a leopard can't change its spots – there are impressive quantities of books. Since I left, my father's turned my bedroom into a reading room. Well, in a manner of speaking: he hasn't actually dismantled my bed or changed the decor, he's simply filled a bookcase with several dozen books that were gathering dust on the living-room floor. He thinks of books as sacred and has always taught me to respect them. I read a lot as a child, less as a teenager, even less as an adult and now not at all with the advent of on-demand TV and the consecration of 'Saint iPad'. Screens have gradually, stealthily replaced books. But they don't smell, they have no texture. I miss paper terribly.

Paper is king in Juliette's world. I want to touch things – and, come to think of it, who's stopping me? I go over to the children's area and find a copy of *Charlie and the Chocolate Factory*. I sit down and leaf through it, stroking the pages. This particular copy hasn't been born yet, it's waiting patiently for the amused attention of a child before it offers up its riches. This young reader will have that unique sensation of turning each new page in anticipation of what's hiding behind it, aquiver with excitement and laughter, and constantly wondering what fresh outlandish adventures the devilish Roald Dahl can have come up with. Many years later that child will still talk about the book with avid enthusiasm, will buy another copy for his or her own children, and will reread it with the obvious pleasure of someone who already knows the story and is passing it on. I close my eyes and I'm five years old again. I can't read yet but I'm curled on my father's lap listening to him read. He was an amazing Willy Wonka with his soft, deep voice. The happiness of this simple scene is still intact, and the images are still vivid. I've always been fascinated by the emotional power of books.

I stand up, run my hands along the shelves and wander around the shop for a few minutes, letting the sensuality of the place intoxicate me. It feels good . . . but this peaceful scene is disrupted by the bell tinkling to announce the arrival of my first customer.

I have the most incredible morning, and I won't apologize for using that word. Everything about this place is a delight. The customers are lovely and very indulgent about my ignorance – I've adopted Juliette's 'We're all allowed to make mistakes, aren't we?', sometimes replacing it with 'We all have a few bloody great gaping holes in our knowledge, don't we!' I get the feeling they leave happy. I don't know if I'm achieving the same turnover as Juliette would but I'm very pleased with my sales of a few contemporary novels. And I now want to read them too. I can't be that bad a bookseller because I'm managing to persuade myself . . .

Bang on midday the bell rings again and someone comes in more confidently than previous customers. Probably a regular. I look up.

It's my mother. Well, Juliette's mother.

My heart beats harder and faster. She comes over, gesticulating and talking to me. I'm anaesthetized, paralysed by my emotions. So this is what it looks like, then, a living mother. Bursting with health, even. Juliette's shown me pictures but in the flesh – with sound and vision – there's so much more to her than any description could conjure.

Paola is . . . how shall I put this? Very colourful.

An Italian accent that's both delicious and disconcerting, sweeping gestures, a wide-brimmed red hat and huge sunglasses that make her look like an actress out for a good time. Quite classy. Which makes the down-to-earth things she's saying and her vast supermarket bag full of Tupperware completely incongruous. Paola is talkative and attentive all rolled into one. She's lovely, really lovely.

'Oh, but you look better, my little weasel! Sorry, I know you don't like me calling you that in the shop . . . but there's no one here so I'm making the most of it.'

She throws back her head and laughs loudly. I reply

with a smile. She rolls her Rs and says 'weaselle', but other words that are often sabotaged by Italians come out perfectly. I mustn't talk too much so I keep smiling. Rule number 1: listen first.

'Has the cat got your tongue? You're normally much more loquacious . . . is that the right word?'

Should I answer that? Yes, here we go, it's my turn.

'We'd usually say talkative, Mum.'

'Yes, talkative, that's it. I'll never get this language right. What can I say, a leopard can't change its spots.'

She starts taking out plastic boxes and puts them on the counter one after the other. There's enough to survive a siege.

'I've made you some Provençal stew with tagliatelle because Marie loves it, some homemade gnocchi (not the filthy stuff they sell in the supermarkets) and a bit of pesto to go with it . . .'

Every time she says an Italian word she lays on the accent. I love it.

'. . . and blanquette of veal. I've also given you some leftover couscous that I froze last week.'

She pauses, peers at me intently, steps close and says, '*Stai bene, tesoro?*'

This is where it gets tricky. Juliette warned me that her mother sometimes talks to her in Italian. I don't speak a word of it. She said I should ignore it and answer in French . . . except I've no idea what she's just asked me.

'Thanks, Mum, thanks so much, this all looks delicious. But it's far too much, you shouldn't have . . .'

'You didn't answer my question. Are you feeling all right? Well, you definitely look better than last week.'

'Yes, Mum. I'm feeling fine. And thanks for the compliment.'

'*Bene, bene* . . . You don't seem to be coughing so much, and your voice sounds clearer too. You see, my essential oils are having an effect, *amore*! Right, I'll go and put all this in the freezer. And it's not really that much for two . . . is Marie upstairs? I can't wait to kiss my little pink pearl . . . then I'd better go, your father's waiting for me and he's double-parked, and he's not exactly patient, as you know . . .'

Your father. Juliette's father. And mine? Images jostle for place inside my head. Emotions do too. Fear, a longing to see him, shame for wishing for any family other than my own father. I pause briefly and lean on the counter to gather my breath, hoping Paola doesn't notice. She watches me, waiting. Oh yes, she asked about Marie. I'm about to reply but she doesn't give me a chance.

'Are you sure you're all right, *tesoro*? You seem strange today . . .'

Shit shit shit shit, Romane, get a grip.

'I'm a bit tired, with this heat . . . but everything's fine, and even better now I've got all these lovely things to eat! Thanks, Mum.'

I move over to her and kiss her cheek. She smiles at me and her suspicions fade. I can breathe.

'And Marie's not here this week,' I tell her. 'She's with Raphaël.'

'Really? Why's she with him? She was with him last week, wasn't she? It should be our turn this week. Sorry . . . your turn. You should spend more time with her. Why are you open on Sundays, anyway? I mean, haven't you got better things to do? Having said that, I noticed you were closed yesterday and I was glad about that, I assumed you were with Marie.'

A mischievous glint flits across her eyes. She steps closer and asks more confidentially, 'But if you weren't with Marie, then who were you with . . . hmm?'

She's making me nervous. I take an imperceptible step back.

'And you're tired today too . . .' she adds meaningfully.

What the flippedy flip can you say you were doing yesterday? Think, Romane, think! No, Juliette, you're Juliette.

'Ha ha. You never miss a thing, do you, Mum! It's none of your business, so far as I know . . .'

I'm trying to play for time but I don't know whether the tone of that last comment is compatible with the sort of relationship Juliette and Paola have. She frowns, peering at me in silence for a couple of seconds. I'm dripping with sweat. Only a few hours and I'm already making Juliette's mother suspicious. She starts to laugh, then strokes my cheek and says that I'm right, it's none of her business, but she's happy to see me looking radiant. A shiver runs down my spine at the touch of her skin; I can't help thinking this may be the first time my mother's laid a hand on me in nearly forty years. My emotions are overwhelming. I try to hide them as best I can, pretending to be interested in something on the screen at the till. Then Paola picks up her Tupperware boxes and heads upstairs to the apartment to put them away.

My brain's in turmoil. I know that Juliette's father is only metres away, waiting in the car for Paola. There's no one in the shop. *Stop deliberating, Romane, if you want to see him, this is your chance.*

Of course I want to see him, this other father. I've hardly thought of anything else for two days. I want to refute the family likeness Juliette has mentioned. Or confirm it. With my own eyes.

I step outside and spot the car that's double-parked. I'm shaking. I knock on the passenger window, a head turns towards me. He unlocks the door and I get into the car, sit in the passenger seat and lean across to kiss him, with my eyes half closed. I automatically give him a 'Hello, Dad,' which sounds false, and he replies with a 'Hello, my darling,' which sounds real.

Gabriel, Juliette's father.

I daren't look at him, even for a second. Everyone

says Juliette looks like him, and the very idea of these shared features terrifies me. So I'm delaying, postponing. I wish I could ask straight out, here in this car, if he's my father, if he's Juliette's father. I wish I could get inside his head to see what's hiding inside there.

Gabriel turns to face me and I look at him at last. I study him in detail.

He asks how I'm feeling in this heat and tells me I'm looking very beautiful. I blush. He also says my mother always dawdles while he's being insulted by hordes of furious drivers, she really does take it too far and has she nearly finished? I tell him she'll be here in a few minutes. An everyday conversation between a father and daughter.

He looks wonderful. The blue of his eyes is very close to mine, true. No freckles but sun-kissed skin, grey hair that's going very white. His face and body look slightly cuddly. He provokes an urge to nestle against him, has a soft, kindly smile. A dream father. Almost perfect. No microscopic canine, though. A certain resemblance, yes, but nothing glaring if you ask me.

I feel strangely relieved. There's still a chance that my real father really is just that. But there's also a chance that Gabriel is.

Meeting him is gruelling. My muscles are painfully tense, I can feel tears welling in my eyes. Juliette's father – *actually your father right now, Romane* – says it's been ages since I've been home for a meal, I should come over one evening, he'd love that.

I need to get out of this car or I'm going to start crying and I wouldn't be able to explain that. I give Gabriel a kiss and open the door just as Paola's coming out of the shop. She scolds me for leaving the bookshop unattended . . . 'And just so you could give your father a kiss . . . not very sensible, Juliette!' If only Paola knew just how sensible I am, just how much I've suffered for it all these years . . . I tell her I was very close by, there wasn't any risk, amazed to hear myself saying these things, a performance worthy of the Actors Studio considering it's not in my cautious nature to believe a word of it, but I've let myself get carried away by my need to meet Gabriel as well. Paola gives me a hug and a kiss, calls me her weasel again, says she'll drop in again on Thursday, and then gets into the car. They each blow me one last exaggerated kiss, Gabriel starts up the car and they're gone.

Back in the bookshop I feel I'm suffocating. I need the help of one of my paper bags to pull myself together. The shop's empty so I sit down . . . and breathe.

I don't know what to think now. There seemed to be a real partnership between them. But exactly what sort of partnership? Is it him? Is it her? *Are you my parents*? I realize I didn't think of surreptitiously taking anything that would have their DNA on it. Well, I couldn't go tearing out a handful of hair; there was nothing I could have done. All in good time. Juliette's at the hospital and I'm helping her, keeping her secret. The other secret – the one about our origins – has been around for nearly forty years so I need to face up to the facts, even if they are painful: this won't happen overnight, I must go about it slowly and not cause anyone any pain by stirring up fear and suspicion. I mustn't damage anything. Just unravel the threads.

Either way, as far as our identity swap goes, I realize I've just been put through a fundamental test and I came out of it rather well in the end. My confidence in our arrangement has shot up: if Juliette's own parents didn't notice anything, everyone else should be a piece of cake. *Oh flippedy flip, you mustn't say that, Romane . . . you need to stay on the alert, don't let your guard down.*

I can't help thinking about Paola and Gabriel for the whole rest of the day. Would I like Paola to be my biological mother? Yes. Given where I've got to in my life, I'd take pretty much any mother so long as she's not dead or a serial killer . . . Do I look like Gabriel? Yes, I think I do. A bit, a lot? Averagely, I'd say. But similarities aren't proof, far from it.

Still, the urge, the need to investigate our origins is eating away at me more and more. I can't talk to Juliette's parents without her, that would be a betrayal. On the other hand, I can do some investigating. I decide to rifle through drawers and cupboards after I've closed the shop this evening. Juliette didn't say I couldn't, after all.

I spend the afternoon in a state of confident vigilance, applying Juliette's instructions to the letter, twiddling my hair and dropping 'obviously' into my conversation when I grasp that a customer is a vague acquaintance. Generally, the people who come in are very nice and very polite. More so than in Paris, I think.

The only worrying episode happens towards the end of the afternoon. A respectable-looking older woman spends a good ten minutes in the bookshop: aged seventy-five by my reckoning, perfectly set hair (white bordering on mauve), Peter Pan collar over a red jumper, and she's wearing tights despite the stifling July heat. I'd like to have a word, warn her that at her age she's risking thrombosis by keeping her legs trussed up in an oven, and thrombosis can lead to pulmonary embolism and death. But I hold back. She seems to be looking for a particular book, picking up several and putting them back down again. I ask if I can help her and she doesn't answer but just smiles. Unsure how well she knows Juliette, I don't want to say too much, I mustn't give myself away. So I keep an eye on her and let her wander around the shop.

While I'm concentrating on the order software as I try to get hold of a copy of Jean Anouilh's *Antigone* for a future literature student, I hear the bell ring and see the old lady slip out rather more speedily than I would have expected of her. I get the feeling she was waiting for me to be busy, for me to take my eyes off her, to *do something*. I suspect her of stealing a book and this upsets me. In my imagination, people don't steal – or no longer steal – at that age. Perhaps I'm naive? Perhaps she's a kleptomaniac? Perhaps I'm paranoid? That last option is a proven fact, the others are less certain. In any event, I'll need to watch her carefully if she decides to pay me another visit.

Apart from this interlude, the day goes by without a hitch. The beginning of my mission has been a success. I have to say I'm rather pleased with myself.

Juliette calls just after I close the shop. Delighted that I can tell her how well everything's gone, I settle in one of the comfortable leather chairs, cross my legs and pick up with a smile on my lips.

My enthusiasm is instantly deflated. What I hear doesn't cheer me at all. Juliette is more breathless than yesterday, more even than this morning. As if just being in hospital and knowing I'm set up in Avignon has released something she's managed to keep in check until now.

The doctors are mystified and she'll be having a day of intensive tests tomorrow. The team at the hospital suspect there's been a sharp acceleration in her condition and, to be sure of their diagnosis, they need to eliminate all other possibilities. I hold back my tears, I must stay strong and send her positive waves. I tell her that everything's fine here and I've *got it going on* (trying to bring my vocabulary up to date). This makes her want to laugh but she can't: with the first 'ha' she starts coughing and succumbs to a long painful bout.

I don't tell her about meeting her parents or my urge – my need – to rummage through our respective lives. I don't have the nerve.

Juliette tells me she's named me as her first point of contact and, as a doctor, I know what this means: I would be contacted by her doctors if there's a problem, and I would speak for her if she was unable to. I would be the only point of contact and would then transmit information to her loved ones. A patient can name whoever they like and doesn't have to justify this choice. As far as the hospital is concerned, I'm Laurence Delgrange, Juliette's twin sister. She opted to give me a false name in order to avoid getting bogged down in intricate explanations and to preserve my anonymity and my real life. Juliette gave them the correct number: mine . . . well, hers – the number of the phone I currently have in my hand. She just asks me to change the voicemail message so that it doesn't use a name. I've already done that.

I can feel fear building inside me and I start breathing

too quickly. I disguise my panic, thinking it grossly inappropriate in comparison with what my sister's going through. Juliette's decision to choose me makes sense because she doesn't want anyone else to know what's going on, but if anything happened to her, I couldn't take responsibility for breaking the news to her family. I tell her – again – that she really must talk to them. If she doesn't do it for her own sake, she must do it for theirs.

'I'm not asking you to tell them, Romane. Don't worry, I'm sure it's not as serious as they think and everything will sort itself out soon. And if it comes to that, then I promise you . . . I'll be the one to tell them. You have my solemn promise.'

My heart is breaking in two as I hang up.

When I'm in Juliette's apartment I open every cupboard in her bedroom and every drawer in the living room but all I find are clothes and boring household admin. On Juliette's computer, I scroll through various files of photos but the scale of the task feels exhausting. Judging by the thousands of digital images stored here, Juliette loves taking photos. I look at pictures but don't know who's who or who I'm looking for.

As I shut down the computer a truly invidious feeling settles in the pit of my stomach. A combination of apprehension, uncertainty and *something else*. It's only an impression – furtive but persistent. As if a shard of truth has wedged itself somewhere into the course of this.

Despite Paola's wonderful gnocchi with pesto, I spend a good part of the evening in tears, wondering what I may have missed.

Wondering whether my sister's going to die and we were destined never to get to know each other properly.

If her diagnosis is confirmed, the inevitable outcome will be imminent.

12

Wednesday

Impromptu no. 1

I wake with a tight knot in my stomach. I really don't feel like opening the bookshop. I want to go and join Juliette, to be with her at such a difficult time. But I know I'm more useful to her here. I can't let her down. I've managed to reason with myself and accept that I must wait. Juliette's young, she can be one of the survivors. I must stay optimistic, keep hope alive, help her turn a corner and get her head around telling her family she has cancer. It's worth my being here for that alone.

The morning is very quiet and I decide to spend it making headway with my investigation. When that word takes shape in my mind, it makes me feel like a sort of phoney Inspector Columbo, but I can't think of another way to describe what I'm doing. I want to get hold of my birth certificate – the real one, because I have my doubts about what my father showed me the other evening. In my Internet research I discover that there are two types of birth certificate in France: extracts and full copies, which may include details of the line of descent. I have to admit I've never taken much interest in them; I've never needed to. I can request a copy of the document on the Internet but the site says the process takes several days. Several days . . . the mental arithmetic doesn't take long: the time it takes for the request to be handled, the document printed and then posted (because they don't send electronic copies), bearing in mind it's the holiday season . . . I'll be waiting a good two weeks. Far too long. I won't hold out till then, psychologically. To get one more quickly I could go to one of the district town halls in Paris where I was born. So that would be the same for Juliette. I'm nearly 700 km from Paris and I'm committed to running a bookshop. I'd have to find a way of leaving the shop for a whole day without raising any suspicion. How the flip am I going to do that? Could I ask Paola to man the shop for me?

During the course of the morning I also have time to log on to the Belgian site running the DNA tests for me. They've received my payment and the samples, and I should have the results in a few days. I'm feverishly impatient.

I wonder what my father's doing at the moment; is he trying to contact me? I have no way of knowing because Juliette has my phone. He tried to call me about ten times on Monday and sent the same number of texts. I imagine he did the same yesterday. I didn't dare ask

Juliette about it; she's got bigger, fiercer fish to fry. I'm annoyed with myself for not giving my father some sign of life. I know he's as paranoid as I am, he must be picturing the worst. But I also feel this little pause could accelerate things: if he's stressing about me, maybe he'll be more prepared to disclose his secrets. I must make a real effort not to contact him before I have the results of the DNA tests. It's only a few days. And if I really can't hold out that long, I'll give Madame Lebrun a casual call, to reassure him and hear how he is but indirectly.

The bookshop is buzzing with customers for a couple of hours over lunchtime. There are about twenty people on the premises the whole time, I'm very much in demand and I make more sales than I did in eight hours yesterday. I'm starving because I haven't eaten a thing since yesterday evening and I'm fantasizing about the blanquette of veal in the fridge. I say no to a text from Paola inviting me to dinner tomorrow and I'm evasive when she asks whether I'll be having dinner with a man . . . she won't give up so I eventually say yes because I hope it will make her leave me alone. Quite the opposite – my 'yes' provokes a call, which I don't answer. Between serving two customers I listen to her message: she's giggly, hysterical, desperate to know everything about this man and says three or four times how wonderful this is. Oh Lord, whatever made me tell her that?

I'm deep in conversation with a customer who's looking for a tourist guide to Provence when I hear a familiar voice. My heart skips a beat. I don't react, pretend not to have heard even though the voice was perfectly clear. Someone's just called my surname. My real surname. Preceded by the word 'Doctor'.

I turn around and recognize him instantly: he's one of my patients.

I ask him to wait a moment, briskly direct the customer to the travel section and try awkwardly to find a quiet corner to talk to this man whose name I've forgotten, though I do remember that he's . . . let's say esoteric. On the other hand, I haven't forgotten his physique, I'd recognize it in amongst a thousand people. He's a little younger than I am, say thirty-six or thirty-seven. Good-looking. Very good-looking. Mixed race. From Guadeloupe, I think, yes, it's coming back to me. Along with his first name: Désiré. You couldn't make it up. Desirable indeed. His face and body are worthy of the men's underwear pages of *La Redoute* – yes, I do like leafing through those pages, thank you – and he has a perfect, almost old-fashioned way of speaking. And he's blind. He's standing here in front of me with his Ultra-Brite smile, his designer sunglasses and his street-art-customized white stick.

'Hello, Doctor. What a nice surprise to bump into you. What are you doing here? Are you here for the festival? Forgive me for being intrusive but I thought I heard you giving advice about books.'

Fucking shitty shit on your grandma's arse. I don't know what to do. If I tell him he's got it wrong and I need to help someone else in the shop, it'll create an incident . . . I'm suddenly terribly hot and short of breath, succumbing to hypoglycaemia. A customer comes over to talk to me . . . Should I ignore her or not? No, I can't. I ask Désiré to excuse me and wait a moment, to which he replies, 'But of course, it would be my pleasure.' I love the way he talks. I'm stressed, I'm all in a flutter, I'm stark raving mad.

I point the nice customer in the direction of the foreign literature section, then turn to Désiré who's standing by the audio books. Even though the city's teeming with Parisians because of the festival, seeing him here is seriously unexpected, a cruel blow.

'I'm afraid I don't remember your name, Mr erm . . .'

'Call me Désiré.'

'Désiré. OK. Tell me . . . how . . . how did you recognize me?'

'I saw you straight away! You're looking glorious, by the way. No, I'm joking. Well, not about you being glorious . . . blind humour, do forgive me. I heard your voice, of course. My hearing's very acute. I always remember a pretty voice.'

I realize that I'm twiddling my hair. Which I never

do, except when I'm in embarrassing situations. But at least Désiré won't see.

'You haven't said what you're doing here,' he continues. 'Have you taken a summer job as well as your practice?'

He can't know this but when he smiles he gets two long creases in his cheeks. No, he must have been told hundreds of times how gorgeous he is and how irresistible those little furrows are.

'I'm here to help my great-aunt so she can get some rest. And it also gives me an opportunity to enjoy the festival.'

'Well, that does you credit. What plays have you seen in the last few days?'

Can't he give up already? Am I asking him any questions, for goodness' sake? Quick, what classic is bound to be in production somewhere among the hundreds of plays in Avignon? Something by Molière. I risk it.

'*The Learned Ladies*. I only arrived yesterday, you know, I haven't had time to see much.'

'Wonderful, what did you think of it?'

He's starting to be a pain now. I need to get rid of him quickly.

'Wonderful, actually. I loved it. If you'll excuse me, it's very busy, I need to . . .'

'Of course, I'm so sorry to have disturbed you. I do love this sort of coincidence. I mean meeting you here like this . . . I can't help thinking there must be . . . a karmic dimension . . . Oh, don't worry, I'm not mad, and that wasn't a two-franc pick-up line . . . I mean two-euro . . .'

He's definitely a bit too talkative but my curiosity about this man – who, like me, seems to be stuck in another age – is aroused.

'I don't know whether I've mentioned this before,' he adds. 'I mean, I only come to you for coughs and colds, after all, but I'm an actor. I'm performing a one-man show here in Avignon. I should very much like to invite you to a performance.'

What sort of shit-fest is this? The man's a flipping fantasist . . .

'I know what you're thinking. You think I'm a fantasist.'

OK, so he's also a mind-reader. Careful now, Romane, stop picturing him in the underwear pages of that bloody catalogue, he might just know you're doing it.

'The blind actor, that's my "hook", a niche no one had taken. At first people come out of curiosity, I realize that . . . a bit like people going to see freaks at fairs in the past. I'm the modern, politically correct version. My job is to make them forget the blind man and see only the actor. I'm performing this evening. Do come, I'd be delighted.'

He hands me an invitation. It all certainly *feels* real.

'I . . . I don't know. I'm not sure I can but thank you anyway.'

'I insist. I warn you, I'm keeping an eye on you . . .'

Pause. Little laugh. It's warm in here despite the air conditioning.

'I'm teasing you . . . that sort of thing makes you sighted people feel far more uncomfortable than it does the blind. I've had nearly forty years to get used to it. I'd better go, Doctor . . . It occurs to me only now that I don't know your first name. What is your name?'

'Juliette.'

'Juliette's a very beautiful name. Very theatrical. Until this evening, I hope, Juliette.'

Why on earth did I tell him my name was Juliette? With that on top of what I told the real Juliette's mother, you could say I'm making a habit of these gaffes. Having said that, half a minute later I realize I was right to give Désiré that name: the moment he's gone a rather tiresome customer comes and starts badgering me. He seems well aware that my name's Juliette and tries to ask me out for dinner. Honestly . . . I've had more invitations in ten minutes than in the last five years. I'm flattered but politely decline. This man doesn't have Désiré's advantages.

Oh, flippedy flip, what am I saying? I need to get a grip. This isn't why I'm here and a pretty boy like that's not for me. Granted, he's blind, but sooner or later someone will tell him I'm nothing special. Then he'll dump me, I'll go into a decline, mope about, and lose six months of my life and five kilos (well, that would be the only positive). I'd suffer like an ageing groupie to see him triumph on stage. Better not to take any risks.

As I think that last thought, I wonder exactly what I'm so afraid of . . . what could I possibly risk when I have nothing to lose?

13

Wednesday

Impromptu no. 2

I block Désiré from my mind and run to buy a sandwich from the bakery opposite. I've got so hungry that I've come up with psychosomatic abdominal pains and started imagining appendicitis, an emergency operation, peritonitis . . . Well, I've definitely been dreaming about a ham baguette for nearly an hour, seeing as there's not time for the blanquette.

The afternoon is exhausting. The bookshop is still just as full but I'm starting to realize I love it, the contact, a little anecdote here, a listening ear there. It's one of my favourite aspects of my work as a GP. And here it is again in this job. Our lives aren't such poles apart as I thought. The same liking for humankind expressed differently in Juliette and myself thanks to the subjects we've studied and our family environments. If my father hadn't pushed me towards medicine, what route would I have chosen? Perhaps this one, who knows?

At about four o'clock a fifty-something man with

dirty grey hair and a matching T-shirt hurries up to me clutching a green Post-it.

'Are you the bookseller?'

'Yes, I am . . . hello.'

'Can you tell me where your "trapper" section is?'

'Um . . . I don't have a "trapper" section, I'm so sorry . . .'

'Damn. You never have anything here . . . I'm looking for a book, you know, it came out this month . . .'

I look at him a little blankly.

'They talked about it on a show three weeks ago,' he continues. 'Don't you watch TV, for God's sake?'

'Um . . . not much, no . . . but which show was it?'

'I can't remember what it's called, but it was on RTL.'

'Ah, well, it was on the radio then?'

'OK, listen, if you haven't got it, you haven't got it, have you, so don't let's make a big thing of this. Could you call the bookshop opposite the town hall to see if they've got it? Last time this happened they had the coffin construction manual that I wanted when you didn't.'

Another blank look from me.

A dazzling opportunity to send a giggly text to Juliette. I don't deny myself this pleasure, transcribing the conversation as faithfully as possible. Juliette's unambiguous reply: *I looooove it* ☺☺☺

*

The strange older woman comes back. Same anachronistic red jumper, same immaculate mauvish hair, same time of day. Like yesterday, she spends about ten minutes in the shop, picking up and putting back lots of books, smiles when I offer to help her . . . and makes the most of a moment's distraction (well, I do have to deal with other customers) to slip away. As she walks past the window she pauses almost imperceptibly and winks at me. Or did I dream that? Who on earth is this woman? I promise myself I won't take my eyes off her for a second in future. If my projections are right, she'll be back at bang on 5.30 tomorrow.

At 6.25 I switch off the lights and wind down the metal shutter. I'm exhausted but I'm planning to do some more rummaging in Juliette's apartment this evening. The strange feeling that I missed *something* yesterday has stayed with me all day. *Something* I looked at without seeing, or listened to without hearing . . . *something* important that snagged at my mind and hasn't let go. Before going up to the apartment I decide to grant myself what I think is a well-deserved break. I'm just heading for one of the comfortable leather armchairs when I hear noises upstairs.

There's someone up there.

I start to panic. My breathing accelerates. I immediately picture the worst, of course. The chances of coming face to face with a burglar, rapist or assassin are extremely small but still far too high for my liking. I grab a pair of scissors and go up the stairs that connect the shop to the apartment. I consider running away but think this through sensibly: if the cause of the sound isn't a crime, my running away would attract attention, flagging up a change in Juliette's behaviour (because I don't get the feeling my sister lives in a permanent state of terror for her own personal safety).

My heart's going to pop out of my chest.

Breathe, Romane. There's bound to be an explanation. Could it be Paola? No, she would definitely have come in to see me first. Juliette herself? She would have warned me she was coming back. Who else has keys to the apartment? Juliette's father? Possibly. As I get closer, the sounds become clearer, more distinct. I'm terrified.

I suddenly hear a child screaming.

No, laughing. Flippedy flip, a child laughing.

That's a relief, but the relief doesn't last long. I now know what's going on because I can also hear a man's voice.

Marie and Raphaël.

What are they doing here? Juliette said they'd be in Nice . . . Apparently not any more.

I have to behave as if I've known them forever – one of them's my child and the other's my ex-partner. My heartrate's reached maximum speed. I prepare a delighted expression. *Not so tense, Romane, more natural.*

I walk into the living room and a little blonde dynamo throws itself at me shrieking, 'Mummy!', jumps into my arms and kisses me. I kiss her back. She smells delicious. A subtle blend of vanilla and candyfloss. I put her back down and glance at the background to this idyllic scene: Raphaël's not quite so great in the flesh as in photos. I go over to give him a kiss. How exactly do you kiss your ex? A standard-issue air kiss to each cheek? Yes, I think so. But there are regional differences; how many kisses do they do in Avignon? Juliette always gives me two. Let's go with two and if that's wrong, I'm up for an embarrassed little laugh.

Marie is already heading off to her bedroom. I notice she's dressed in pink from head to toe; they've got a thing about pink in this family. Raphaël's been spared the sweetshop attack: he's wearing dark jeans and a close-fitting petrol-blue polo shirt. He smiles at me. I went too far just now – jealousy, probably – he's really not bad at all. Dark eyes that make him look intelligent, a narrow nose, slight greying at the temples. He's still smiling, one of those smiles that begs forgiveness for something. I'm worried because I can guess what he's going to say. (I'm not completely stupid.)

'I'm really sorry I didn't call, Juliette, we had to come back from Nice in a hurry. I had a call from Olympia, they urgently need a sound engineer for the next four days. If I turn this down, I'll end up with a lot of people in the profession on my back . . . I've got a train in an hour. Could you have Marie, pleeease? It was your week, anyway . . . If you can't, maybe your mother can help?'

A glitch. A massive one.

I don't know what to say. Juliette's told me very little about Raphaël because I wasn't meant to see him. All I know is they separated relatively amicably three years ago and she likes him. She said she's no longer in love with him but seemed very happy that their relationship is still good. She told me they both want Marie to be happy and they have no trouble making harmonious arrangements.

I feel trapped . . . so that's what I say.

'I don't seem to have a choice . . . It's not very convenient . . . When will you be back?'

'Monday.'

'Monday! But you said four days.'

'Four evening concerts starting tomorrow, which means I get back on Monday.'

'And you're sure there's no other way you can work this?'

'Fuck's sake, Juliette, come on. When you asked me to have Marie a couple of days ago, I agreed without asking why. If I don't take this job, I'll be blacklisted by those producers. And then I'd definitely have lots more time to look after Marie . . . but I don't think that's what you want for me, is it?'

He's put out. The vice is tightening. I'm cornered.

'That's not what I meant, Raphaël. I understand . . . of course I'll have Marie. I'll manage. You go and don't stress.'

'You're the best, thanks, my Jules.'

He leans over and gives me just one kiss on just one cheek. I blush and turn away to hide my emotion.

Raphaël says goodbye to Marie and promises these few days will go by very quickly. She puts her arms around him and coquettishly says, 'I'll miss you, my darling Daddy,' which makes me think Oedipus still has plenty of mileage left in him. Then she goes back to her room hollering the hit song from a Disney film about ice princesses so sweetly that it would drive the most fervent republican to loathe any form of freedom.

Which is how I end up with a pink five-year-old girl.

I can feel a great wave of stress rising inside me, along with total euphoria.

After all, I'm a mother for the first time.

[illegible]

[illegible] That's not what I'm not [illegible] understand. Of course I'll have [illegible] and [illegible]

[illegible]

[illegible] She [illegible] her arms around him and [illegible] Try [illegible] my [illegible]

[illegible] freedom.

[illegible]

After all, I'm a [illegible]

14

Wednesday

Marie

How long have I been obsessed with the idea of being a mother? I can't possibly pinpoint a specific time it started. The longing just always seems to have been there.

As a little girl I played with dolls, like everyone else. I also pretended to be pregnant, like lots of other girls. I role-played as a mother taking care of her babies – always girls, and always two of them. I've never thought about that before but my plastic offspring always came in twos. Two sisters. It's not that they were twins, I don't think that was it, but in my games I was systematically mother to an inseparable pair. I don't believe in coincidences; I believe in the subconscious, in traces left by past events. I think I appropriated what I myself had experienced, snuggled against my sister, in the first nine months of my life. I think I incorporated it into my games without even thinking about it. Nothing happens by chance.

I desperately wanted to be a mother. I never found

the right partner and refused to use a casual fling as a gene donor. Perhaps I was wrong. I think everyone has a right to give their love to a child, everyone is capable of that. Whatever their background, their community, sexuality, religion or allegiances. And it doesn't matter whether the child is theirs naturally or by adoption. There's so much suffering among adults and children, and bringing two instances of suffering together can produce staggering examples of filial love. Put like that, it might seem a bit clichéd – I do realize I sound like an aspiring Miss World giving her interview on the night of the finals . . . but that really is what I believe in my heart of hearts.

I grew up in a family that is now referred to by that terrible term 'single-parent'. Single-parent doesn't mean half as much love, quite the opposite. It means just one parent day in, day out: twice the responsibility for one individual. I've never felt up to single-parenthood, I've never taken the leap.

I haven't given up but I have come to terms with the situation. And now, at thirty-nine, I find I have a niece, and this evening – for perhaps the only time in my life – I need to be her mother. To pretend. Play the part. Can I do this? I know absolutely nothing about real children. Confronted with pretty little Marie, I feel quite out of my depth. She's irresistible, of course, but I'm so unsure of myself.

Marie doesn't ask my opinion: she hasn't seen her mother for a week so she's got some catching-up to do.

I take a deep breath, abandon my idea of rooting around like a knock-off Sherlock Holmes, and throw myself wholeheartedly into what will prove to be one of the most wonderful evenings of my entire life.

*

We spend a few minutes chatting and joking, and Marie draws me into her world; at first I feel like an intruder, flitting from one surprise to the next, but I gradually succumb to it and can feel myself letting go.

She explains earnestly that she's just started what she calls a 'pink week'.

'I saw it on YouTube, it was really really funny . . . you have to wear pink and eat pink things all week, you're not allowed any other colours, except a bit of white, and some red too 'cos it's nearly the same . . . Will you help me, Mummy, pleeease?'

'Um . . . but it's not possible to eat only pink things for a whole week. What did you eat with Daddy?'

'Well, I had ham and strawberry milk and raspberries and prawns . . . he got some sushi too . . . and also he made normal stuff to eat but he added strawberry sauce or a colour-making thingy . . . we had a pink omelette, it was yummy!'

I decide to take the easiest option and head out with

Marie to find some sushi – I would have thought it was unusual for a child to like it but I'm lucky: Marie loves it.

Along the way, Marie tells me about something she'd like us to do together – something I could manage if I take a Xanax beforehand. I tell her about the obvious risks of this enterprise but she corners me.

'You're funny sometimes, Mummy . . . why're you suddenly frightened when it was your idea? We'll play the game like last time, and only stay in one place, OK? It was really really fun, I really really want to do it again . . . Go on, Mummy, say yes, please please please . . .'

This tirade is paired with huge, imploring eyes and a completely adorable mock-praying pose. I concede but without naming a day, thinking that Juliette will be back in the meantime.

We keep walking for a moment and then I reconsider. I ask Marie to wait a moment and she dawdles, gazing at the countless posters for shows, while I type away at my phone looking for the vital information: yes, it's open for another hour and a half, and yes, we have time to go there.

This may be your one and only evening as a mother, Romane. Might as well make the most of it. Take a deep breath, stay calm, have a muscle relaxant, and then . . . flipping well go for it!

'Change of plan, little lady. Follow me!'

Marie's eyes light up.

'Where we going, Mummy?'

'We're going to take a taxi.'

'A taxi? But why not the car?'

Because you'd be bloody terrified if I were driving, sweetheart.

'The car's broken down, I couldn't get it started this morning. So we're taking a taxi, which'll be fun, don't you think?'

'Mmm-yeah . . . and where are we going, Mummy? Oh, please tell me, please! 'Cos I'd like to stay at home playing.'

Doubtful little pout. Hangdog eyes.

'It's a surprise, I can't say a thing . . . but I promise you we'll have a great time.'

I take Marie towards the ramparts, on the outskirts of the historic city centre, where we find a taxi rank.

I slip a piece of paper to the driver who pauses and mutters that it's definitely the first time anyone's asked to go there by taxi, and called it a 'surprise' . . . specially for a child. I'm tempted to tell him to mind his own business but settle for, 'Trust me, she's going to love it.'

As we draw closer, Marie recognizes the car park and starts whooping for joy and kissing me.

'Amazing!! Thank you, Mummy, it's going to be brilliant!'

The driver throws back his head and laughs, saying he'd never have guessed a little girl could get so excited about going to IKEA. I tell him my daughter's exceptional and that's all there is to it. Marie's over the moon.

We spend a good half-hour in the bed department and Marie insists we do 'exactly the same as last time', which involves me hiding under a bed with one foot sticking out and waiting till a salesman spots me. Marie roars with laughter from where she's waiting in ambush under the next bed. When the sales assistant leans over and asks me if everything's all right, I say that of course it is, I was just having a little nap! I come out of hiding, high-five Marie and head off to the wardrobes area. We choose a nice big one, take up our positions inside it, try to silence our giggling, and wait a few minutes. The sound of footsteps, a sales assistant waxing lyrical about the PAX system used in conjunction with HOKKSUND sliding doors. Marie and I put on extravagant eagle masks that we dug out in the children's department and that glory in the name of LATTJO, then we raise our arms and hook our fingers into talons to ensure we're truly terrifying. When the wardrobe opens to reveal our B-movie horror scene we both laugh sardonically like the baddies we are. A chubby woman gives a piercing scream, calls us every name under the sun: I mean, what a stupid thing to do . . . So we take off our masks and race breathlessly to kitchen utensils where we hide behind a rotating display unit showing off a flan dish. There we catch our breath and discuss the success of our exploits. Marie's bent double laughing, and I'm nearly in the same state myself, but we have to sneak away because I get the feeling several sales assistants have us in their sights . . .

*

Back at Juliette's apartment after a nice meal of sushi, Marie leads me into her bedroom. It's already gone ten o'clock but she's on holiday, and I so want to spin out this evening with her that I've agreed to delay bedtime again. She peers at me with a look of great concentration: there's nothing more serious than a game – Marie knows this, and she's going to teach me.

She gets me to sit down facing a little gaggle of cuddly toys and dolls. I can see a dolphin, a princess, a hairy little monkey that goes by the name of Kiki, a rabbit with ears as long as its body, a pink-and-green dragon, a Paddington Bear with a red hat and blue duffel coat, and a unicorn.

'So there are two teams,' Marie starts to explain. 'There's a princess and her name's Lisa. She's with Dolphin and she's in prison with her pet Zebulon.'

'Which one's Zebulon?'

'Don't be silly, Mummy, Zebulon's Zebulon, here,' she says, pointing to the brightly coloured dragon. 'Have you forgotted him?'

'Of course I haven't . . . So you're that team, and who am I?'

'Well, I think you were doing Kiki . . . and the others

can be guards,' she explains, gesturing towards the dolphin, the unicorn, the rabbit – Noonoo to his friends – and Paddington.

'Noonoo's name in the game is Chloe,' she goes on, 'and the unicorn is Lally. They're all guards and all of you want to steal the princess, and I stop her getting out of prison.'

The story makes no sense at all. I love it.

'Mummy, you know Lally's my favourite teddy, she really is, honestly honestly, you gave her to me when you went to Rome with Nanny Paola . . . she's my bestest teddy . . . thank you, Mummy!'

She throws her arms around my neck and hugs me before segueing straight to something else.

In the end the game's very easy for me because it's a monologue on Marie's part. I watch her closely and ask a few questions, all of which she answers with feigned exasperation, as if I'm really very tiresome because I don't understand a thing. But when I ask if she'd rather play on her own, she gives me a forthright scowl.

'No, why did you say that? I like playing with you best! Let's carry on. Are you listening?'

'Of course I'm listening, sweetheart. I was watching you and I just . . . I thought how beautiful you are.'

'Ah. OK. But at the minute you're trying to steal the princess with your guards and then another one comes along to save me, and it's Kiki because he used to be in love with me but he didn't tell the others . . . do you understand, Mummy? And then . . . well, we'll see what happens then.'

This child is glorious.

I've known her for less than four hours and I already feel boundless affection for her. As if my whole body recognizes her. Marie. My niece. You're so like your mother. You're so like me.

I can feel my tears welling.

'Are you playing, Mummy? Come on, you've got to be the guards now. Go ON!!'

My eyes are glistening but I start to laugh.

'What's the matter? Why're you laughing? It's not funny. I'm the princess and I'm going to get caught . . . and now Zebulon's starting to get worried . . .'

I pull myself together and concentrate on this captivating adventure.

'Where is this prison?'

'Well, it's here, in this box.'

'But isn't the princess happy in there . . . ?'

'Um, people aren't happy in prisons, Mummy, are they? . . . OK, you're taking too long so let's say everyone from the castle came and the princess got married to Kiki and they took lots of photos at the end.'

She picks up a toy smartphone and mimics someone taking pictures on their mobile.

'And are they happy afterwards?' I venture.

'Of course they're happy. Look, they've had a baby, it's Zebulon. They'll be together forever.'

She puts the little dragon between its two parents and I have to hold back my tears. I'm no therapist but this whole story reeks of subliminal messages. I feel so close to her. And I dearly wish I could have a reconstituted family too.

'OK, Mummy, can you do the music for the end now?' she says, interrupting my thoughts again.

'No, you do it. You sing so much better than me.'

What was I thinking! Inevitably, she plumps for the same song with the princess hollering how happy she is to be free.

*

Just before she goes to sleep, Marie asks me to read her a story – Tomi Ungerer's *The Three Robbers* – and then asks for a hug. Which is the most inexpressible pleasure for me to give her.

'We had the best time this evening . . . Thank you, Mummy. I missed you, you know. I love you.'

'I love you too, my sweetheart.'

'It's funny when you call me sweetheart, you never call me that. But I like it.'

Oops. What should I call her again? The same nickname Paola uses for Juliette, I think.

'It's good to mix things up from time to time, don't you think, my weasel . . .'

Marie gives me one last smile, I turn out the light and slip out of her room.

I'm exhausted. I head for the living room and drop down onto the green velvet sofa. This apartment's very nice, a bit too untidy for my liking but as warm as its inhabitants. The temperature's perfect – I think the heatwave is over.

I have a new text from Juliette. A couple of hours ago I let her know that Marie was here, and apologized for not calling her for obvious reasons of secrecy. She replied saying she quite understood and was very sorry that Raphaël couldn't hold on to Marie . . . Naturally, I asked how she felt, and how her tests are going.

Her reply's just come in now.

Not feeling great, but OK. Results tomorrow, at the earliest.

Then a second text.

Romane, I wanted to say. Everything you're doing for me is so wonderful, I'll never be able to thank you enough. Thank you from the bottom of my heart. Big hug to both of you.

Those last words are overwhelming.

I reply simply: *Juliette, your daughter's incredible. She adores you. She needs her mummy. We miss you. Come back soon, my sister.*

THAT NIGHT

From the first moment I knew I couldn't love her.

Twinhood is a cancer. It stole my childhood and now it wanted to steal my future.

I sat on the floor again with you in my arms. I hugged you closer to me.

Leaving the other one to squall.

And with those screams my whole childhood resurfaced . . . along with all its disasters.

*

I was brought up by a powerful mother, a painter who was always the centre of attention, leaving no space for anyone else. My father – who was also a doctor, no one escapes their destiny – was unhealthily reserved. Pathologically self-effacing. I've never understood how two such different people ever came together. I think my father loved my mother, admired her, worshipped her. And my mother loved the adoration heaped on her. Otherwise, she didn't really care. Him or some other man, it didn't matter.

My mother subsumed my father, rode roughshod over my childhood. She was strong. In every sense of the word. A towering presence. I should have been too, but I was always the puny, sickly, bespectacled boy at the top of the class. I know she was ashamed of me – she loathed weakness. If I was bullied in the playground, 'Well, you must have asked for it, and you need to learn to defend yourself!' If I had a bad mark for my work, 'What have I done to deserve a child like this!' If I had a temperature that just wouldn't drop, 'Oh, you're so clingy, ask your father to look after you, and leave me in peace with your whingeing!'

I hated her exuberance, her fanatical selfishness, her shamelessness, her loud laugh when she picked me up from school. I so wished she could be like my classmates' mothers.

My mother was the albatross around my neck, but she was my mother. I spent my childhood begging for her smile, for a sign of interest. And I got them occasionally. They're hoarded in my memory, still vivid. But most of the time she couldn't care less what my father and I did or thought.

The only man who found favour in my mother's eyes, the love of her life, was her brother. Her twin. A twin she loved unconditionally. All-embracingly. Overridingly. A twin who was more important to her than her husband, or her son. Who never gave way an inch to anyone else. My father and I were no match for him. It was an unequal battle, the dice were loaded. He had more than thirty years' lead on us.

I remember one episode as if it was yesterday: waiting for my mother outside school for two whole hours in driving rain, in the middle of winter. A kindly old lady scooped me up and called my father who came to collect me without a word of comfort for this poor shivering child with a face ravaged by fear and tears. My mother had forgotten me, and my father held his tongue, it was as simple as that. I was eight. On that particular day my mother had raced off to be with her brother because he was very low – he'd always been depressive, and he put this angst down to the physical distance between him and his sister, to her marriage and motherhood. It broke my mother's heart to see her brother suffer and she would fly to his bedside. Seeing her son suffer left her cold, indifferent. I always knew my mother's relationship with her twin wasn't normal. I've always thought twinhood was an absolute bitch.

When this beloved brother died in a motorbike accident my mother's life fell apart. And so did ours. She descended into deep despair. It went on for many painful weeks, with my father and I taking turns to try to entertain her and brighten her mood. Nothing helped. Nothing. And one morning she took her own life. She preferred death – abandoning her husband and son – to a life without her brother. I was nine.

My father gave up. With hindsight I can see that he'd already given up while my mother was alive, but I didn't understand it so clearly at the time. A year went by, with my father doing the barest minimum. I lived in a degree of material comfort, lacked for nothing. Except for love. I tried to piece myself together single-handed, stranded between bitter memories of my mother and the realities of a father who got out of the house at the first opportunity. A passive father, whom I also hated, because he was incapable of looking after me, of giving me the attention I so desperately needed, and always had. A father who lasted only a year without my mother. Who decided to finish it all too. I was ten.

I ended up with my paternal grandparents. They were old, destroyed by grief. They did what they could. They were there for me. They gave me a home. Compensated. My wounds were deep and I kept my distance. But I loved them. My grandparents weren't talkative or demonstrative, they were like my father in many ways, but I know they loved me too. We all need to love someone, otherwise how do we cope? What made my parents' deaths unbearable was my acute understanding of what their suicides meant: they didn't love me enough, or they would have stayed. My grandparents saved me.

I always promised myself that when I had a child, I would be the exact opposite of my parents. I would be overflowing with love, involved, there whenever I was needed. I've always thought that when it comes to parental love, too much was much better than not enough.

I was a young medical student when I met your mother. I fell hopelessly in love with this girl whose personality and physique were so exactly the opposite of my own mother's. She was everything my mother hadn't been: disarmingly dainty, smiley, gentle and attentive. She loved me and admired me. I loved her and admired her. That was the happiest time of my life. When she told me she was pregnant I felt as if I was living a fairy tale and I was rising from the ashes of my childhood.

The day she died I lost everything. My wife, my love, my dreams, my longings.

*

When I found her dead that day I could see history repeating itself. Twinhood, which had been so destructive for the little boy I'd once been, jumped out at me. It was right there in front of me, all over again. Guilty, all over again.

I instantly knew that if she hadn't been carrying twins, she would still have been alive. If that other baby hadn't been there, your mother would still have been with me. Twin pregnancies are much more dangerous. Special vigilance is needed during delivery: there are many more instances of haemorrhaging with twins. If I'd known, I would never have left her alone in that deserted building. The guilt will be with me for the rest of my life. The same what-ifs will keep coming back for the rest of my life: 'If I hadn't been on duty . . . if the building hadn't been empty . . . if the phone hadn't been cut off . . . if she'd been carrying just one baby . . . if I'd known . . .' How could I have known? Her pregnancy was normal and your mother had the best care available in 1975. Five years, ten years later, scientific progress and the wholesale adoption of ultrasound scans might have saved her. Or perhaps not. Nothing's ever been infallible. And it may never be.

I was instantly gripped by a radical, indescribable feeling of horror. My daughters might grow up loving each other beyond all measure like my mother and her twin brother, with such a symbiotic love that anyone else – even their own father – would be excluded. I know just how impenetrable that twin-world can be; the pain of exclusion is engraved deep inside me. I knew I wouldn't survive it again. It would kill me. I had to break the cycle. At any cost.

I instantly made the decision. It was inescapable. Visceral.

I needed to act. And quickly.

I cleaned the baby without really looking at it, and wrapped it in a blanket.

I swaddled you warmly in the soft sheets that had been bought for you and nestled you up against your mother.

In a quick fifteen minutes I'd be back, alone.

Before going out with the other baby, I decided to give her a name. I have no idea why. Perhaps to connect her symbolically with your mother. Her mother. Of course, we hadn't planned for her. She hadn't been a part of our lives, our plans. She wouldn't be a part of mine. But a little voice deep inside me whispered that your mother, the love of my life, might have accepted her. I remembered our second choice, a name I didn't much like but your mother did. Her choice. Not mine. Not ours. I scribbled it on a scrap of paper and slipped it under the thick blanket.

I went out into the cold and the snow with the tightly bundled baby. I kept glancing around, starting at the least noise, but the roads were deserted.

I knew where to go. There was a convent only three streets away. I would put the baby on the steps. I don't believe in God but I had an outdated image engraved on my mind: nuns would never turn away a baby abandoned at their door. Particularly on a night like this.

I put the child on the bare ground; it was terribly cold so I knew she wouldn't last long. I had to be quick. I knocked on the huge door, powerful thudding knocks. Then I ran off, pulling my coat closer around me and burying my face between my shoulders under cover of the dark, dark night. It felt like being in a film. I was tormented by fears. What would happen if anyone saw me? It was 1 January 1976, it was snowing, the temperature was well below zero; no one would see me.

I watched from a distance. If nothing happened, how long should I leave it before going back for her? And what other options would I have then?

All at once there was a creak. I held my breath, darted around a corner where I couldn't be seen. The door opened. I heard a cry of surprise, and then whispering. Several women's voices. A few footsteps in the snow. None close enough to make me run for it. I waited a little longer. At last another, muffled sound. The door closing. The baby had stopped crying. Silence settled. For good. I craned my head around the street corner where I'd been hiding. The door was shut, the baby had been taken in.

I started to shake. Violently. With cold. And fear. And shock.

The full horror of what I'd done suddenly struck me. The guilt too. Sobs swelled in my chest. I succumbed to the tension that had accumulated inside me. I was no longer sure I'd made the right decision.

I took a few deep breaths and pulled myself together, summoning a mental picture of my mother who had died of her excessive love for her twin. And then my tears stopped. Yes, I'd done what had to be done.

I wish you a wonderful life, little girl, *I thought almost out loud,* but I'm not the person to give it to you. I just can't.

I had to act quickly then, there was no time to think.

I ran through the snow, my fears mounting as I climbed through the floors of our still woefully deserted building.

I washed you and wrapped you in blankets. The nicest ones I could find.

I laid you down next to your mother and settled you, yes you, our daughter, in between us, in the crook of her arm. I knew it would be the one and only time the three of us would be together. I wanted it to go on forever. I hugged your mother. Kissed her. Said goodbye to her. For all time. I don't know how long I stayed there like that.

My heart, my body, my mind – all of me had been destroyed, consumed.

Before leaving the apartment I had the presence of mind to clean her body a little and remove the placenta with its two tell-tale umbilical cords in order to throw it away in some anonymous dustbin. Wiping away any trace. Rewriting history.

I arrived at the hospital with you, telling everyone what I'd just been through. My sobs building as the horror of the situation came back to me: I arrived home, my wife was dead, she'd haemorrhaged after delivery, there was nothing I could do, the phone was cut off, I had to deal with it on my own, I'd taken the time to wash this woman I loved so much, to restore her dignity, and I'd taken care of my daughter, then I came here. End of story.

Colleagues of mine – obstetricians and pathologists – would cast their kindly professional eyes over your mother's body and come to the same conclusion. No one would ever question my decision to wash her or to deal with the placenta. I wasn't just some patient in that hospital, I was one of the team. They all knew I'd spent the day with them. They all understood my suffering, my pain, what I'd done. They all supported my decisions. Decisions taken in desperate circumstances by a man, a doctor, who had lost his own wife. A man destroyed by grief.

No one would ever question my version of the facts. They were as remorseless as they were painful. An excruciatingly ordinary perfect storm of circumstances.

As ordinary as death.

My version of the facts became the only version, the only truth.

Until I chose to reinvent it.

15

Thursday

Dead ends

Marie's in the bookshop with me this morning, and Paola's coming to pick her up at about eleven. She's a very calm child but she's also very talkative. I know the shop's much busier in the afternoons so it would be difficult for me to keep an eye on her. And there's no question of letting her out of my sight for a moment. What if I relaxed my vigilance? She could be kidnapped or have an accident . . . I don't even want to think about it. And even though I adore the child, I'm secretly hoping Paola can have her until Saturday morning.

All through the night I went over and over the various possible scenarios of Juliette's and my origins, and I considered what I'm allowed to do without her consent – or what I will allow myself to do. I'd like to talk to Juliette's parents, to tell them everything with no filter, to bombard them with questions until the truth emerges. But I know that's impossible. It's up to Juliette to ask them all the questions that are eating me up, I can't take that away from her. I don't think I could bear it if she asked my father questions instead of me. Our pact is one of emotional stability. The undertaking I made was to preserve the happiness of Juliette's loved ones until she has a clearer idea of her condition. If I cross a line, I know I'd destroy everything: the trust she's put in me, our love for each other (so new but already so powerful), her hopes, her life. I must be reasonable and wait a few more days. That might seem like nothing after thirty-nine years, but it's an eternity . . .

There are two things I can do, though. The first is to get my father to speak, by going about it calmly and thoughtfully this time, smoothing the sharp edges and apologizing for things I said the other evening that made him fly off the handle in a way I've never seen him do before. Telephones are out of the question for a conversation that important: I need to go to Paris. And while I'm there, I can do the second thing: get copies of our birth certificates, mine and Juliette's. In two different town halls, armed with our respective IDs – Juliette left me her ID card just in case . . . she didn't know how helpful she was being. It's only four days since I met my sister but waiting another day to have these precious documents in my hand – I'm sorry, Juliette, I just can't do it. I'm going to close the shop tomorrow. One little day to find out so much more. To brush aside some of the theories with the flick of a rubber stamp. To lift the hazy veil over our lives, whether what we find is wonderful or appalling. Not just for me, for both of us. I hope she'll understand. I'll explain this evening, on the phone. Or not. I haven't decided yet. I'm not sure I want to cause her any additional stress. Maybe it would be better to tell her what I've done when I'm back from Paris. When I know more.

Marie is sitting at the desk in the children's area, drawing and humming – still, inevitably, the same song. She's happy, anyone can tell. I think I could spend hours gazing at her if I didn't have far more compelling thoughts buzzing around inside my head.

The old lady comes into the shop again at about 10.30. The same ritual as before, just a few hours earlier than I'd anticipated. I watch her and she smiles at me. Marie looks up after a few minutes.

'Hello, Madame Racine,' she says.

'Hello, Marie,' comes the reply.

I'm rooted to the spot. They know each other. Which means I'm supposed to know her, obviously. And I've been thinking of her as a stranger for two days. Marie comes to give Madame Racine a kiss, then goes back to what she was doing.

Madame Racine comes closer to me. Her smile is different, more enigmatic. She waves me over, leans towards my ear and whispers, 'I know you're not Juliette.'

Did I hear that right? I've turned to stone. I glance at Marie but she's engrossed in her drawing and not paying any attention to us. I try to sweep aside what Madame Racine has just said with a quick riposte.

'True, I've put on a bit of weight . . . but it's not very kind to point it out like that, ha ha . . . How can I help you, Madame Racine?'

'You're not Juliette and I know who you are. I won't breathe a word. I just wanted to say that it's amazing, what you're doing for your sister. I'm sure God will reward you.'

I have to cling to the thrillers table to stop my legs giving way. I need to end this conversation.

'God's got no business in all this, Madame Racine,' I whisper urgently. 'And I don't know what you're talking about. Now, I'm sorry but I have a couple of orders to place.'

'Of course, I didn't mean to get in your way. Don't worry, your secret's safe with me. I've known Juliette for years, you know. She's a wonderful woman. I hope with all my heart she'll pull through this.'

I stand there speechless as Madame Racine leaves.

How could she know? No one, not even Juliette's own mother, has noticed our deception. I'm shaken, shocked, appalled. The confidence I've built up in the last two days has just been atomized. If Madame Racine knows, then other people may know too. What did I do wrong? I spoke to her too soon, got the tone of voice wrong, treated her like any old customer when she's a regular.

I've fucked up, big time. Or . . . could Juliette have confided in this woman? Maybe, but then why didn't she tell me? I need to know for sure. I text Juliette, asking whether she told Madame Racine about our arrangement. I wait a few seconds . . . but I won't have an answer straight away. Of course Juliette's not glued to her phone. I hope she's feeling all right this morning.

Marie comes up to me and I take a deep breath.

'Are you OK, Mummy? You look funny.'

Get a grip, Romane, for goodness' sake.

'Of course I'm OK, I'm very OK, my weasel. How about you, what are you up to?'

'Here, this is for you.'

She hands me a drawing of the adventure we acted out yesterday evening: I recognize the little dragon in the arms of a princess and another animal . . . probably Kiki.

'Thank you, my lovely. It's brilliant! You were right, they do look happy with their baby dragon.'

No response. She's already moved on to something else.

'Did Madame Racine leave a letter today, Mummy?'

What does she mean? Is Madame Racine the postie? A bit old for that, I would have thought.

'I . . . I don't think so, sweetheart.'

'Come on, let's look for it. Which books did she touch?'

Marie takes my hand and I show her which row of books Madame Racine walked down. She starts taking volumes off the shelves one after another, opens them to the first page, then puts them back. She's very excited. I'm about to ask her what she's up to but she's already talking.

'Do you remember the letter she put in a big book of photographs of Paris? I think Madame Racine writes beautiful things. But sometimes the words are all a bit complicated for me . . . Aaaah, there's one in here!'

Marie has just taken an envelope from a copy of Virginia Woolf's *Mrs Dalloway*. She hands it to me, asks me to open it without tearing it – Madame Racine wouldn't like that, and we need to put it back where it came from when we've read it.

I open the envelope carefully. Inside it I find Marguerite Yourcenar's poem 'You'll Never Know', and I start reading it out loud.

As I read my vocal chords constrict. I think back to the way Madame Racine strolls around the shop and leaves without buying anything. I thought she was a thief but she's actually a poetry smuggler, a literary bootlegger, leaving deeply affecting offerings inside books. I've never seen it happen but can only imagine the little hit of happiness that these anonymous gifts give to readers: they'd be surprised, amused, perhaps moved, definitely intrigued. Juliette's life certainly is full of surprises.

This missive is intended for me, I'm sure of that, particularly the last line: 'And you live on in some small measure because I still live.' Madame Racine knows about Juliette and me. If I had any remaining doubts, this poem has just eradicated them; especially the last verse. Was Madame Racine sent by Juliette herself to make me reconsider her suggestion that I should replace her completely if anything happened to her? Does Juliette feel she's closer to the end than she's implied? I glance at my phone. Still no reply.

Marie can tell my emotions are running high but can't possibly know what's playing out here.

'Hmm, that's not the best one we've had, is it? Sometimes Madame Racine puts funny stuff, but this one's not brilliant . . .'

I don't have time to think. I put the envelope back inside *Mrs Dalloway*, close my eyes and drink a glass of water. As I put the glass down I see two people coming into the shop. Horror of horrors: it's Paola and Désiré.

At the same time.

They're even being all courteous with each other about who should come through the door first.

They both head towards me.

I thank heaven that I told Désiré my name's Juliette, but I'm still terrified he'll call me 'Doctor', in front of

Juliette's mother. I need to get each of them on their own, be one step ahead of them, and definitely not call Paola 'Mum' because I'm meant to be in my great-aunt's shop and he could easily know my mother's dead, a lot of my patients do . . . I'm not sure Désiré is one of them but I can't afford to take that sort of risk.

I go over to Paola first, give her a quick kiss and say that I need to take care of my customer. She elbows me, saying he's not a bad-looking customer and is he who I'm seeing this evening? Flippedy flip, she's right, I'm meant to be out tonight. I tell her this evening's been cancelled and, anyway, I have to look after Marie – even though I was planning to ask her to have Marie for an extra day. When I'm out of my depth I mess everything up. And I'm flat-out panicking right now. I absolutely must keep Paola away from Désiré. I nudge Paola towards her granddaughter, and she's only too happy to oblige: she hasn't seen the child for ten days and was already hoping for a cuddle forty-eight hours ago.

I go back over to Désiré and say hello but in a way that makes it clear I'm busy. When he speaks, his eyes – which are hidden behind blue-rimmed sunglasses – are angled just above my head as if he imagines I'm taller than I am. *There are lots of things about me that wouldn't measure up if you could see me, believe me . . .*

'I don't think you were there last night, were you?'

'No, you're right. I had . . . a bit of a mishap. But don't worry, I will come to the show.'

'This evening? Do come this evening, please.'

'Ah, this evening's tricky . . . I have to look after–'

'No, she doesn't! She's absolutely free this evening!'

Paola has just muscled in on our conversation. This sudden intrusion is extremely unpleasant but, more importantly, it's dangerous. It would only take a misplaced 'Doctor' or 'my daughter' to produce a nuclear explosion. I need to say something to Paola but I can't call her Paola or Mum . . . it feels like I've hit a wall.

'I'm taking care of Marie this evening! We've got so much catching-up to do and we're going to have a lovely pink girls' evening, aren't we, my weaselkin? Don't you worry, Juliette, you have a nice evening with Monsieur . . .'

I'm stuck in a dead end. Again. I need to end this high-risk conversation as quickly as possible. I suddenly have a flash of inspiration.

'Great . . . Marie can spend the night with you, but I won't be able to come and pick her up tomorrow . . . could you possibly have her till Saturday morning?'

Whoops of joy from my niece and her grandmother, jubilant acquiescence from Paola and a victory dance from Marie.

'And I'll come to see your show this evening, Désiré.'

Sneaky smile from Paola. She doesn't know that I'll

steal away, and neither does he. What matters for now is that everyone believes I'll be there so this dangerous conversation can come to an end.

'I think I owe you a thank you, madame. Your intervention was perfectly timed . . .'

'The pleasure's all mine, dear monsieur. Particularly as you have such a delightful name. It's always a pleasure to see Juliette in such good company.'

She gives me an extremely explicit wink and breaks into a loud laugh. Anyone would think she was flirting with him . . . He pretends to apologize. His smile's a killer, Paola's right about that.

'I feel as if I slightly forced your hand, Juliette . . . as an apology, I'd like to offer you lunch.'

Oh, come on, how much more of this is there?

'That's very kind but no thank you, I need to stay in the shop, I'm open non-stop at the moment.'

'Don't worry about *that*!' Paola pipes up. 'Oh, you can be boring! Marie and I will look after the shop, *tesoro*, while you go and have lunch together. Look, there's no one here, we'll manage very well, won't we, Marie?'

Marie nods enthusiastically. Paola is actually a pest! She's good at this. I've been backed into a corner and I really need to get Désiré away if I'm going to avoid a total disaster. So I reluctantly accept this invitation that I really could have done without, particularly as I haven't been alone with a man without a stethoscope around my neck for I can't remember how long.

I look at my phone before going out. Nearly an hour and still no reply from my sister.

I know there's nothing remarkable about waiting that long but Désiré's lovely smile can't quell the gnawing anxiety that's worming its way into the darkest recesses of my mind.

16

Thursday

The beginnings of a bridge

We walk through the streets of Avignon and my awkwardness is palpable. I haven't walked side by side with a man for centuries; I don't know what to say to him and I don't want to be here at all. In other circumstances, I'm sure I would have appreciated Désiré's company but this really isn't the time. My mind's focused on my trip to Paris this evening, on the conversation I'll have with my father, and on Juliette. I've got my phone readily accessible and keep checking it because my sister's silence is worrying.

Désiré navigates with perfect ease through the city's streets even though they're very busy. If it weren't for his not-really-white white stick or his stately head carriage peculiar to the blind, I think his disability would be undetectable. He smiles, makes a few mundane comments about the weather, the heat, the very distinctive mood in Avignon at this time of year, and how much he loves the festival and theatre in general. My replies couldn't be briefer. I have one simple aim: to curtail this 'date'.

'Listen, Désiré,' I manage eventually. 'I don't know if you're coming on to me but I'm not interested. I'm not . . . in the right frame of mind. So could we please just pretend we've had lunch together and stop now. It would be better for everyone.'

He stops, turns to face me, smiles and leans in slightly.

'Listen, Romane . . . because your name *is* Romane, isn't it?'

He pauses. I can feel my pulse pounding in my temples. I start to shake. I'm about to say something but he cuts in.

'You seemed . . . strange yesterday. And I had a vague recollection of your first name . . . not the one you told me. I'm naturally inquisitive so I dug out an old prescription from you, a friend kindly read it for me and confirmed what I suspected. You haven't denied that you're my GP so it seems that that's who you are. But you gave me a false name. No, don't say anything . . . let me keep going, if I may.'

I'm completely paralysed. I don't know what to say.

Think, woman, flipping well think.

'It felt to me as if you were trying to keep me away from your great-aunt just now,' he continues. 'Or is she your mother? Given the nature of your conversation, I got the feeling the little girl was yours and the Italian woman your mother . . . What this all boils down to is . . . I don't know exactly what you're hiding but I'm sure there's something. And I'm intrigued. In a positive way. You know, I do like actresses, whether they're professional or playing a part . . . as an amateur. I love the thought that you're by turns a doctor and a bookseller, a Parisienne and an Avignonnaise, Romane or Juliette. It's all fiendishly exciting. I promise I won't say a thing. If you honour our dates, of course.'

I'm flabbergasted. I've thrown myself straight into a trap, and I can't see any way out. The biggest problem is that I've dragged Juliette and her silences into it too. I'm suddenly struck by the truth of the situation: what Désiré is doing is despicable, that's the only word for it. It's blackmail, plain and simple. I won't give in to his offensive 'if you honour our dates' . . . I'm not prepared to go to any lengths to keep this secret, I won't prostitute myself, what was he thinking? And I tell him as much, using those very words.

'Whoa, now, let's calm down a bit,' he says. 'Please don't misunderstand my intentions. No, this isn't blackmail . . . After all, you accepted my invitations without a knife to your throat. We all have our dark side, a secret garden we want to keep from prying eyes, not allowing others in. I thoroughly respect that. I know you're not entirely who you claim to be, and that suits me. I wanted you to know that I like you. I already liked you when we were doctor and patient, but I never had the nerve to admit it, that's all. I just felt that this chance encounter in Avignon was a sign and that I had to take the initiative, I had to ask you out . . . I was wrong. If you find my company so repellent, I shall yield. I won't beg for your time or your attention, I've never done that and I never shall. Don't worry, I won't contact you again. And I'll change doctors, I promise. Goodbye, Doctor.'

He moves away. He's going. Flippedy flip, he's really going. He's upset. He's gorgeous. I'm attracted to him. I don't find him repellent, quite the opposite. It's just that this really isn't – and I mean *really* isn't – the moment. OK, but when would be? I'm thirty-nine years old, I'm desperately lonely, the whole world's lied to me about my life, my twin sister might be about to die . . . when will I think the time is right enough to start living?

'Wait!'

I realize I just shrieked that. He stops. Turns around but doesn't walk back. It's up to me to take a step towards him. Symbolically as well as literally. I take the step.

'Désiré . . . I'm so sorry. I didn't mean to . . . I get things so wrong, please forgive me. When I agreed to this . . . date it was because I really wanted to.'

A pause. He's facing me. Reaches out his hands. Takes hold of mine.

'You're shaking, Romane. It is Romane, isn't it?'

'Yes.'

'You're shaking. I take that as a sign of sincerity. This may seem strange to you but our hands betray us just as often as our voices. They have a life of their own. Of course, we can control them . . . but they also harbour many of our emotions. Yours seem honest to me. I'm glad you've agreed to open a chink in the armour protecting you . . . it's protecting you but it's blocking your access to some people, and some feelings. And I think you have a right to them.'

We're so close together it feels as if he's going to kiss me. It feels as if I would let him. He doesn't move, though, obviously. But something's just happened, here, in the middle of this noisy crowd. Something with an electric, mineral quality.

I take a deep breath and start to laugh. It's like a sea wall giving way. Désiré laughs too, still holding my hand.

'I have an idea,' he says and he leads me away. He seems to know exactly where he's going, his blindness doesn't stop him moving at a speed that I have trouble matching.

We make our way through the narrow streets and I think I properly take on board the reality of the Avignon Festival for the first time. I haven't really paid any attention to it so far. As I carve through the crowd with

Désiré I notice everything. My senses, which have been numbed for too long, are emerging from their torpor.

All through the streets of Avignon thousands of posters for performances are plastered in every direction: on walls, streetlights, nylon wires strung between buildings and on shopfronts. A wonderful mosaic full of eye-popping colours, attention-seeking slogans and groan-inducing jokes. And they match the exuberant bustle, the singing, laughter and applause that captivates and sets alight the whole city. I'm struck by the fact that everyone around me seems happy. Avignon in July is a bubble of theatre set apart from normal time. For a few hours or a few days, each person puts routine life on hold to receive or administer intravenous exultation. The 'nurses' are actors, performing extracts out in the street to attract their patient-spectators to their show. It's a powerful dose with an intense adrenaline hit and instant visible effects.

I ask Désiré whether he also uses this tactic – which is actually very charming – to persuade punters to come to see him. He replies, almost ashamed, that he doesn't really need to, his show was sold out by 1 July, having had a lot of buzz when he performed in Paris in the winter. *Flip, so am I the only person who doesn't know who this man is?* Now that he's told me this, I reinterpret the way passers-by keep looking at him . . . both men and women. I thought I'd noticed people staring at us a bit, and I put it down to that sort of voyeurism that draws the eye to anyone out of the ordinary. I suddenly realize that it's not just because Désiré's blind that he gets noticed, it's also because he's famous. Well, I can't be sure he's truly famous, but let's say quite well known in the theatre world, as far as I can make out.

'Your hand's gone all tense, Romane . . . I can tell that you have no idea what my performance entails . . . and that's perfect. That's exactly one of my key criteria. I'm joking, by the way. Although . . . Anyway, I'd really love to invite you into my world, that's why I offered you a ticket for this evening.'

He slows down. There's definitely nothing run-of-the-mill about this man.

'We're here, Romane!'

I look around. OK . . . we're on a bridge. Désiré is sitting on an ordinary bench on an ordinary bridge with ordinary cars driving by.

'Wait, don't give up on me yet . . . I know what you're thinking . . . *This chap's completely mad, he asks me out for lunch and then takes me to a bridge which isn't even the famous Avignon bridge.*'

'I have to say this place is . . . how shall put this? Original, that's it. And we haven't got anything to eat, which – I'm sure you'll agree – is a bit confusing for a lunch.'

'Ah, but you're wrong! I have the makings of

sandwiches plus beer and water in my backpack. We have everything we need.'

I now wonder whether he's utterly and completely mad . . .

I sit on the bench, close my eyes and try to let go but the sound of traffic swishing past only a couple of metres away is deafening. And cars can so easily skid off the road . . . Désiré has started making sandwiches. He hands me a beer and raises his.

'To our meeting, Romane.'

'To our meeting. But . . . if you don't mind my asking, why've you brought me to a bridge?'

'Because there's nothing better than a bridge . . .'

Silence. Hesitation.

'I can just imagine what you're thinking. Let me explain, Romane. Bridges are like a concentrate of life. It's all there in a bridge. The option to choose one direction or its exact opposite, the whole tumult of human life, of course, and then just a few metres below, the power of nature, a river that can carry us to even further destinations. Different worlds. Bridges are exciting, mysterious and infinitely precious.'

He pauses. I don't know what to think. I'm not as poetic as he is. To me, a bridge is just a bridge. Some steel, some concrete, cars, danger, noise, and that's it. I tell him so and he starts to laugh, a genuine, sunny laugh.

'Right now, you're wondering how you can get away from this complete nutcase without risking your life . . . Will he throw you off the bridge in the pursuit of his experimental ravings?'

He pauses again but he's still laughing. He's definitely full of surprises.

'Don't you worry,' he says, moving a little closer. 'You're not in any danger with me. I just love bridges. When I was growing up in Guadeloupe my father used to take me fishing and we'd sit on the wall on the edge of a bridge. People in our village were horrified that he'd let me sit on the parapet like that, risking me falling off and making it into the local paper. The poor little blind boy carried off by the river . . . Everyone else around me wanted to put me in a protective cage. It was well intended but really stifling. By letting me sit on that bridge, my father made me feel nothing was impossible for me and the whole world was within my grasp. I could live like other people. But to do that I'd have to go beyond the boundaries that they set for me. We spent hours there. It was on that bridge more than anywhere else that I learned to sharpen my hearing. And it was on that bridge that I listened as my father read plays from the French canon. It was also on that bridge in the Guadeloupe countryside that I chose my path in life. Treading the boards, under the lights. Turning my back on darkness, whatever the cost. I was born on that bridge. As I said, Romane, a bridge has everything in it. You can even hear the beat of your own heart, if you concentrate hard enough. I thought you might find something here too. I don't know what you're looking for, Romane, but I have a feeling you're very nearly there.'

I have an irrepressible urge to cry. *Flipping shitty bridge.*

Why am I so moved by what he's just said? Is it the way he's opened up, the frankness veiled in clouds of metaphor and memory? Is it his voice, which manages to be both very deep and very gentle? Or the things he doesn't say but that I can read in his expression? Is it the burdens from his childhood, the way other people viewed him and the serenity he's achieved as an adult having found his way thanks to that little bridge in his home country? Is it the contrast I can sense between his father and mine? How can the same force of love produce such different results? On the one hand, instilling such total confidence in a blind boy that he comes up with this insane desire to parade himself in front of everyone, while on the other burying a perfectly healthy child under layers of fear, anxiety and paralysing phobias.

Désiré doesn't know me and I don't know him, and yet it feels to me as if we've already come a long way. Far beyond this bridge.

I eat the sandwich he's made for me and we chat about everything and nothing, his work, and his show – which I'm meant to be seeing at six o'clock this evening. He says that he will perform it for me, and I say he must have told dozens of groupies the same thing, and he says he hasn't, and I'll soon see just how wrong I am.

As we talk, I can feel the knot in my stomach growing. The feeling I had two days ago – the sense that I missed *something* – nettles me again. I try to concentrate on what Désiré's saying but I'm more and more distracted, and he notices.

'Is something wrong, Romane?'

'No, no, everything's fine . . . it's just . . . a strange feeling. Could you . . . you're going to think I'm very odd . . . could you repeat what you've said in the last five minutes?'

'Um . . . well, I've said quite a lot in five minutes . . .'

He pauses for a moment. Smiles.

'You're different, aren't you. So, let me think . . . I was banging on about my life in Avignon, saying I got here at the end of June and first I had a few days' break before starting rehearsals . . .'

'Keep going, go on, please.'

'. . . then I said rehearsals ended on 6 July and my performance is at six every evening because in Avignon there are shows non-stop all through the day. I said early afternoon is often a good time for a walk, which is how I came across the bookshop in the first place. One day when I was walking past I heard voices and laughter coming from the shop. There was a reception laid on for a book signing, but I think it was the popping of champagne corks that lured me in. I also said I'm a big fan of audio books and the last one I really loved was . . .'

Blah, blah, blah, blah, blah, blah. I can see his lips moving but I've stopped listening. I concentrate. The feeling's there again. It's getting stronger. I'm so close to my goal. Oh flip, what's he saying?

I concentrate again but that makes the feeling dissipate. It's getting away from me.

Fucking shitty shit shit, I'm going mad – no, I think I already am.

I thank Désiré with one kiss on the cheek, although I'm not sure what I'm thanking him for: the lunch, the bridges, this *something*, or something else altogether. So I thank him for everything.

'Oh, don't thank me, there's no need, really. See you later, Romane?'

'See you later, Désiré.'

Despite all the warring emotions throwing me into turmoil, despite everything that feels like a higher priority in my life at the moment, I know I will go to watch his performance when it comes down to it. Because the truth is, there's nothing to stop me. Because I want to.

Because it's wrong to turn your back on a spark of life. Because it's my choice, and far too many decisions have been made for me up till now. Because I'm my own bridge, and because unlike Juliette, I'm incredibly lucky that I can still choose which way I want to go.

Is this what it feels like, then, deciding to live for your own sake?

17

Thursday

Lights

In the afternoon, alone in the bookshop after Marie and Paola have left, I rest my head against my folded arms and close my eyes. I think about letting myself sleep – which would be madness because the shop's open – but the uneasiness is still there. All at once I get a sense of it, that unsettling feeling, though I don't know where it's originating from.

So far, I've put my trust in Juliette almost blindly, on the basis of the incredible likeness between us. But I don't know anything about her. And I can't be sure she's as honest as I am. Is Juliette lying to me? *Something* has put that idea in my head. The *something* I can't quite pin down.

Is Juliette manipulating me? Is Juliette a very good actress who's used her supposed love to snare the poor mousy creature that I am? Is she playing an active role in the lie that I'm perpetrating? Why would she lie to me?

Juliette is off-radar, she hasn't replied to my messages. I'm worried but I'm also getting things in perspective.

Maybe her illness is just a front . . . I'm instantly angry with myself for this uncharitably inappropriate thought. It doesn't stand up to scrutiny. Everything about her seems so real. I'm a doctor, I know her cough was genuine. Harrowing. Of course, there could be all sorts of causes for it, but why would she let me think it was cancer if that wasn't the absolute truth? Why would she have gone to the pulmonology department of the Hôpital Nord? And that's a proven fact too: her health card was definitely there. I'm not sure of anything any more. I don't understand a thing.

I try to call her again. Voicemail. I need to talk to her. Should I go to Marseilles instead of Paris? But if Juliette's been lying to me, what's to stop her lying again? She could be anywhere in that case. This isn't the time for words, it's the time for evidence. I need facts, concrete facts. I click on the Belgian company that's running the DNA tests . . . still nothing. *Flippedy flippedy flip flip.*

I close the bookshop earlier than usual and pack a bag for Paris. It's the best way to achieve something tangible. Getting my hands on our birth certificates is becoming increasingly urgent. Then I'll present them to my father and I won't leave him alone until he gives me an explanation. He can't wriggle out of it this time.

As I walk out of the door I think of Désiré, and that bridge. For a moment I tell myself that, in the midst of all this chaos, something wonderful could happen. And nature always finds its way, even surrounded by concrete. Is it crazy to want a few morsels of happiness just when everything around me is lies and make-believe? But maybe I don't give a damn. Nothing about this situation is normal.

And so I head off to Désiré's show. I'll catch the last train to Paris at twelve minutes past eight.

*

Every seat in the auditorium is taken. There are people begging for more. I'm in the back row with my small suitcase beside me.

The performance blows me away.

Désiré is incredible. He has a knack for stirring emotions in the whole audience. His show isn't a comedy – when he told me it was a one-man show I immediately pictured roars of laughter, I wasn't expecting this. It's his life, as told by him standing on the stage. There's laughter, yes, but there are tears too, and tension. In places it's tough, in others uplifting, often amusing. At the end of the short performance – barely an hour but dense with emotion – I elbow my way to the stage door and realize just how much younger and more beautiful than me all the women waiting for autographs are. I'm about to leave but he catches hold of my arm before I've even moved.

'Don't even think about it, Romane. I'll be all yours in just five minutes, don't stand me up, please.'

I wait. It's 7.20. Five minutes is still doable. When he joins me he notices the sound of the wheels on my suitcase.

'You're running away again, Romane . . . Am I allowed to know where you're going?'

'I'm not running away . . . I need to . . . go to Paris. There are things I need to sort out.'

'That's all very mysterious. Couldn't you . . . delay your trip? I . . . I've cancelled what I was doing this evening. I thought I'd ask you out for dinner. Not on a bridge, though.'

'No.'

'No . . . and that's it?'

He starts to laugh and I realize I've been rude. I'm so focused on what's happening next that I've forgotten the most elementary courtesy.

'I'm sorry, Désiré, I'm not very good company this evening.'

No reply. He's stopped walking and a big smile spreads over his face.

'I'll come with you.'

'Thank you, but no thanks. I'll manage on my own.'

'Let me come with you, please.'

Is it all that obvious that my refusal wasn't heartfelt? I thought Désiré meant he'd see me to Avignon station but in the taxi it becomes clear that he means all the way to Paris. I protest vigorously, for real this time.

'Listen, Romane, I'm a free citizen in a free country . . . I have every right to want to spend time on a high-speed train too, if the fancy takes me. I don't have a show tomorrow . . . and I'm going to tell you my huge, guilty secret: I'm crazy about buffet car sandwiches. As far as I'm concerned, they're the pinnacle of French gastronomy.'

He laughs happily to himself about his own jokes. I resist a little longer, for the sake of appearances, but I think I'm already smiling.

'Be careful, Romane, I can hear you're smiling. And I like it a lot.'

Désiré and I buy last-minute tickets, with seats in different parts of the train but that doesn't matter, we just won't sit down.

This journey is taking me back for another confrontation with my father and with truths I'd prefer never to have to face, but with the help of a few mini bottles of wine and a salad as plastic as its container, I stand in the buffet car laughing and admiring villages we hurtle past, forcing myself to forget just for a few hours the filth I've discovered under the overpolished surface of my existence.

With Désiré everything is disarmingly easy. He doesn't ask any prying questions about me, about all the lies he's flushed out or my reasons for rushing up to Paris. He tells me we have plenty of time. He's right, I think. And yet, standing there with my plastic cup in my hand, I decide to tell him everything. I don't know why. Well, I do . . . because Désiré seems kind, because I can't take much more of carrying this weight on my shoulders and not being able to share it with anyone, because I need a safety valve and he agrees to take on the role. Because he's still smiling at me, in spite of everything. Because he encourages me, helps me to see things more clearly, pushes straight through open doors and opens others that were closed. Because I'm terribly alone and he's here, when he could so easily be somewhere else.

I'm unsteady on my feet when he drops me outside my apartment in Paris. By the front door he kisses my forehead as a goodbye. It makes me shiver despite the heat still gripping the city so late at night.

Once inside my apartment, I collapse onto my starchily new sofa and burst into tears.

I'm almost ashamed of the paradoxical, indecent hint of happiness that flickers when I'm with Désiré, and I cry about this for many a long minute.

In the last few days I've cried the equivalent of ten whole years' worth of tears. I've lived the equivalent of ten whole years' worth of life too. Everything has accelerated. Life, meeting people, feelings, death. It's too much for someone who's never lived this intensely. I'm amazed I still have a supply of tears.

Then I briskly pull myself together. I think about my sister; there's still no news from her. What would Juliette want for me? She'd want me to live, she'd want that desperately. So much so that she's asked me to live for her.

Right now on this Paris night I wish my mother were here with me. I wish my father were here with me. I wish my sister were here with me. And I wish not one of them had ever lied to me.

It's appalling, all the love that once existed but is no longer there. There's nothing more ephemeral, when all is said and done. So we have to know how to grab it when it's there. That's what I tell myself now.

18

Friday

Registrars

The weather in Paris is gloomy on Friday morning. Very different from the day before. The sky is laden, the clouds low. I'm almost cold. I have a slight hangover but I'm not convinced that alcohol is the real cause. I haven't slept all night. Instead of restorative sleep, I had hours of anxiously anticipating the day to come. Until it drove me out of my mind.

My breathing problems and my hypochondria are at their worst, so bad in fact that I'm starting to worry I haven't had an accurate diagnosis. Could I be really ill? Physically, I mean. Mentally, there's some chance, but I'm not the best judge of that.

I've done a lot of thinking in the night. I'm convinced Juliette's not lying. Her surprise when she first saw me was genuine and her symptoms are real. If I haven't managed to get hold of her before early afternoon, I'll go straight to Marseilles from Paris to find her. I need to know. Even if it means breaking my heart.

During the night I also reached a decision not to force

anything on Juliette. Whatever I find out about our beginnings, I'll only tell her things she wants to know. I'm not sure she wants to know the truth, deep down. The lies are so beautiful.

She'll decide for herself, but I'll decide for myself too. And the truth is within reach; I've made the decision to throw myself off the metaphorical bridge and into the river.

I come out of the building in sunglasses, in a hopeless bid to hide the bags under my eyes.

I've walked only a few paces when I hear Désiré's voice. I freeze. Turn around. He's holding a little bag that looks exactly like the ones they have in my local bakery.

'Good morning, Romane. I know how much today means to you and I'm guessing you haven't slept very well so I thought a few morning treats might lift your spirits.'

I feel like crying, again. I don't think anyone apart from my father has ever brought me croissants. My voice sounds strangled when I thank him.

'Romane, I was thinking that . . . perhaps you might need some support. I don't want to force myself on you but I hope you know I'm here if you need me. And I don't have anything better to do today, so . . . Sorry, I don't mean that you're a fallback plan, that's not what I meant at all . . .'

Silence. He's embarrassed, I'm embarrassed, we're embarrassed. I get a grip on myself.

'No, I understand, Désiré. Don't worry, I'm used to not being plan A . . .'

'Romane, genuinely, I didn't mean–'

'I'm teasing you, Désiré. You don't have a monopoly on humour, do you?'

How did I dare say that to him? I'm surprising myself these days. The old Romane would never have blurted out something like that. But the old Romane no longer exists, so I start laughing and he joins me. I take a warm croissant and bite into it. Désiré's right, this is how life should be. I should listen to my own instincts for once, so I let down my guard.

'I . . . it would be really kind of you to come with me. There are some formalities I need to go through, as you know. You'd be very welcome.'

'Perfect. I shall hope to be worthy of your expectations, my dear Romane.'

He mimes a sort of bow, rather as he did to Paola in the bookshop, and hands me the bag. I've always thought of croissants as a sort of drug. I'm reminded of the woman who works in the bakery on the corner of my street and her constant refrain of, 'A croissant's the thing to give your life zing.' I think this incongruous slogan reassures me right now.

A few minutes later I'm in the registrar's department

of the Tenth Arrondissement's *mairie*. No, I don't have an appointment. It's for a birth certificate. No, not an extract, the full copy. Juliette Delgrange, D-E-L-G-range like a range cooker. Yes, I'll wait, thank you.

I've decided to start with Juliette because I'm so terrified of what I'll find and I'd rather be my father's daughter for a few more minutes.

When it comes to my turn everything happens very quickly. The man dealing with me is in a hurry, slightly cross-eyed with a menacing expression, tobacco-stained teeth and no time to waste on niceties – or a smile, it seems. Désiré is right beside me.

'What can I do for you?'

'I need a full copy of a birth certificate.'

'Yes, I got that, madame, but what's it for?'

'I don't understand your question . . .'

He looks at me with exasperation and starts again, enunciating clearly as if I were a child and he a bad-tempered teacher. His mouth opens wider, revealing more of his teeth which seem to be harbouring half of his breakfast. I stifle a retch.

'Who's asking to see this copy? I don't imagine you want it to put it in a frame. I need to know why you're requesting it. Most people only need an extract, you're asking for the full copy, it's part of the procedure to record what you need it for.'

I feel a complete fool: he's right. I don't know what to

say; why would anyone need a full copy of their birth certificate? I haven't the first idea.

'I . . . it's personal. I need it for personal reasons.'

'Well, that's not one of the options, I'm very sorry . . .'

I'm about to say something else when Désiré intervenes.

'Tell him, darling, don't be embarrassed . . . I'm so sorry, my future wife can't quite get her head around the fact she's about to marry someone disabled like me . . . she should have told you from the off that we need it for the wedding. We're getting married in six months' time, at my home in Guadeloupe.'

I stare at him in amazement. Did Désiré plan for this meeting during the night? Or did he just know that a marriage was a legitimate reason to get hold of this wretched bit of paper? Either way, his spiel has completely wrong-footed the man serving us, whose face constricts into a grimace that I can't decipher. I'm just transfixed by his teeth. I think I'd probably die of septicaemia if he suddenly decided to bite me.

'Well, madame, you mustn't be like that. I won't congratulate you. Marriages are built on honesty. Take my wife, she always talks of me with great pride.'

Embarrassed silence. Désiré – the man really is incredible – quips with such a resounding 'And we can see why!' that it sounds true. The civil servant with the papier mâché smile bares his full set of teeth and sniffs robustly as he clicks and types at his computer. Then he stops dead, reads what's on the screen and sneaks a glance at me. He repeats the operation three times . . . and can't disguise his surprise.

'Madame Delgrange, could you tell me about your parents?'

Something's not right.

'I . . . Paola and Gabriel Delgrange, who live in Avignon.'

'Yes, I know that. Um . . . is there anything you'd like to tell me about them?'

'My wife – I'm sorry, my future wife – was adopted. She's ashamed of that too, so she doesn't shout it from the rooftops.'

'Aaah, OK. But your husband's right, you know. You mustn't go around being ashamed of everything like this, or you'll never get anywhere. My wife always says that what she really loves about me is–'

'Don't let's go into details, please . . .' Désiré laughs with a conspiratorial twinkle that obviously has sexual connotations. The man gives a hearty snigger. I'm very worried I'll be spattered with his spit so I recoil slightly. But Désiré has succeeded: the man asks us to wait a moment, hands me back Juliette's ID, asks me to sign – and this I have prepared for – and bids us goodbye, telling me I should definitely hold on to this fiancé of mine who's clearly wonderful-despite-his-handicap.

I'm lost for words, but I'm holding a vital piece of paper in my hand.

Once we're back outside, Désiré bursts out laughing.

'My word, things are moving quickly between us, aren't they, Romane? I mean, we're as good as married now!'

'How did you know? I mean, about marriage and getting hold of a full copy?'

'You mean other than consulting the web page for Paris registrar's offices that deals with administrative formalities? Even with the terrible synthetic voice on my screen-reader software it wasn't that difficult . . .'

He's laughing at me, obviously. At my lack of preparation. I'm definitely a rubbish investigator. I thought of myself as a sort of sub-Sherlock but I'm really a slightly tipsy Miss Marple.

'And why did you say I was adopted?'

'Forgive me for intruding but I could tell you were about to launch into God knows what sort of explanations . . . It was obvious that there was something unusual about your birth certificate or he wouldn't have asked you about your parents like that. And, judging by what you told me yesterday about your family background, I thought that the most likely way to get the man to hand over the certificate would be to mention adoption . . . elementary, my dear Romane.'

Désiré gives me a huge triumphant smile.

My face is in tatters, though.

While he's been talking I've read Juliette's birth certificate.

Her truth is right here before my eyes.

I think about how she'll react when she knows, and tears well in my eyes. *If and only if she wants to know, Romane, remember that. You mustn't force anything on her.*

Four decades of lies are spelled out in calligraphed letters before my misty eyes. Désiré can tell I'm distressed and steps closer, asking me what I've discovered.

Juliette, my sister.

Born 1 January 1976.

Adopted by Paola and Gabriel Delgrange on 14 May 1976.

There the word is, associated with two people who've loved her so dearly for thirty-nine long years that they haven't managed to tell her the truth. I resent them for it, I hate them for doing this to her. I hate them for everything they'll destroy in her heart, in her life. How can you ever trust again when the people closest to you have deceived you?

I try to understand. To guess. To imagine . . . Paola and Gabriel's unhappiness because they couldn't have children. The joy when Juliette came into their lives. A perfectly healthy child. So young she would never remember the months she spent without them. A child who would grow up – and this must have brought further happiness – to look a little like Gabriel. Their decision to move to another city, be surrounded by new neighbours. To start over, as a family of three. The child was theirs. No one would take her from them. Why break her heart, why break their own hearts, already so battered by the pain of waiting for a child that never came, when the solution was right there and so easy? A little lie. As straightforward as Paola's smile in those old photographs showing her stroking her rounded tummy, cherishing a two-hour pregnancy that was so natural, so true that she wished it had gone on forever. A tiny little lie. They'd just have to make a point of handling any requests for official documents and no one would ever know.

Gabriel and Paola Delgrange are not Juliette's parents.

So they're not mine either.

I don't know whether I'm crying because of Juliette's pain or my own. The possibility of a mother whisked away. So abruptly. So cruelly.

Who are we?

This discovery about Juliette reactivates my urgent need to find out about myself.

Désiré suggests a break, stopping for a glass of beer, water, strong spirits, anything to relax me, to *perk me up* – I love the way he uses such old expressions that they could be my own. I refuse but he does insist that I lie down on a bench and do some breathing exercises. I try to empty my mind along with my lungs, and don't really succeed but, in spite of everything, I manage to regulate my breathing.

While I'm pulling myself together, Désiré talks me through the knowledge of registrars' departments that he acquired overnight. He's being annoying but I have to admit that what he's telling me is quite useful. He lists all the documents I can get hold of with just my ID card: my own birth certificate, both my parents' birth certificates and their marriage certificate . . .

'Thank you, Désiré, but I think this masterclass would have been more useful *before* my first dealings with a *mairie*.'

'So, I save your skin and that's all you can say in reply . . . that's a bit much, isn't it?'

I think he's right but I don't have the time or the inclination to be tactful.

We enter another *mairie* with great determination. It's the one for the Nineteenth Arrondissement, just opposite Buttes-Chaumont park. I know the building is magnificent with its columns, arcades and various allegorical statues but I don't see any of that. I'm not here as a tourist.

Registrar's office. Birth certificates. Mine and my parents'. My parents' marriage certificate too. Yes, the full works. Yes, I'll wait, thank you.

This time we're served by a delightful woman who

reminds me of the singer Nana Mouskouri, perhaps because of the shape of her glasses.

'We're here for all the basics. My father's apartment's had a lot of water damage, all his archives were flooded and he's lost everything so he's asked me to get copies of his birth certificate and my mother's and their marriage certificate.'

'Oh, that's terrible, your poor father, I'm so sorry to hear that. I hope he's all right.'

'Yes, it's been terrible. But he's fine. They're just things, he's dealing with it. Thank you for being so kind.'

After some searching and a bit of printing, Nana Mouskouri hands me an envelope containing my parents' whole lives summarized in three certificates. She's definitely more helpful than her opposite number. I clutch the precious envelope feverishly to my heart. It gives me strength to keep going.

'We're also here for another very simple thing: my own birth certificate. A full copy. For our wedding. Our forthcoming wedding.'

I glance at Désiré who's beaming at me with his most convincing smile.

'Oh, how lovely, congratulations!'

'Thank you, thank you so much.'

We're old hands at this but we don't let it show. I start to relax, insofar as that's possible. Nana Mouskouri asks us which *mairie* we'll be using for our wedding and

Désiré tells her it will be at Morne-à-l'Eau in Guadeloupe. He starts to describe its picturesque charms but the woman doesn't take her eyes off her screen, settling for a polite smile.

She doesn't ask any questions.

Désiré turns to me and I notice a slight tensing in his features.

Why's she not asking any questions?

'There we are, that's that. I've emailed your full birth certificate to the registrar's office where you're getting married. There's nothing more you need to do, that's all in order. My best wishes to you both, goodbye.'

We stay rooted to the spot. Nana Mouskouri stares at us with a smile that seems to say, 'I think we've said all that needs to be said, you're free to go.' But we don't go.

'Is there a problem?' she asks.

'It's just . . . I thought you'd give me a copy of the certificate so that I could send it . . . and also so that I'd actually have a copy, in case I'm asked for it again . . .'

She starts to laugh.

'Oh, don't you worry about that. I can assure you no one will ask you for a full copy of your birth certificate. Everything's done electronically these days, hardly anything on paper any more, it avoids a lot of headaches. Even with inheritance issues, we email everything to the solicitors. It makes life much easier for everyone.'

I'm stunned. I can feel a stealthy rage building inside me. *Breathe, Romane, breathe. But don't get out a little paper bag, for the love of God.* Désiré's lost for words too. I need to get on top of this.

'But your colleague at the *mairie* in the Tenth Arron–' I break off mid-sentence. I can't tell her than only an hour ago I was asking for a birth certificate in someone else's name in a different registrar's office.

'My colleague at the *mairie* in the Tenth Arrondissement . . . ?'

'Yes . . . he was . . . very accommodating for my husband. My future husband. He gave us a paper copy of my future husband's birth certificate, no problem.'

'Forgive me, but I thought you said that he was born in Guadeloupe, in Morne-à-l'Eau to be precise?'

Silence. She stares at me, waiting. I need to do something. Now. I take my phone out of my pocket and before she can stop me, I'm behind the desk next to her.

'What have you . . . ? What are you doing, madame? You have no business here! Stop, no, you can't come round here, what do you think . . . ? Security!'

Once I've got what I need, I grab Désiré by the sleeve and drag him out of the building at a run. I know it's unkind to do this and he stumbles badly three times but I save him from falling and we manage to get away.

We run until we're out of breath, into the depths of Buttes-Chaumont park. The place where my father has worked his whole life. Somewhere I find reassuring, where I feel grounded. That's why I chose that particular registrar's office. In a world that's pitching and rolling in every direction, I need a few branches to clutch hold of – otherwise how will I stop myself going under? Désiré doesn't ask any questions, he just keeps chuckling and saying I'm unbelievable. I think he knows what I did.

I have in my hand a photo of Nana Mouskouri's computer screen.

I hope it's not out of focus.

We sit down on the slightly damp grass. The park is virtually deserted on this grey morning. Désiré asks me if I'd like to be alone, and I say no, definitely not. I'm terrified.

I take out my phone. Click on the picture.

I take a deep breath, then hold the air in my lungs.

I skim through the basic information and, just for a moment, I think my world has stayed on an even keel. I let out the air. I can breathe at last.

I swipe my fingers wide to zoom in; I think I know what I'm going to read.

But I don't know anything. I've never known anything.

I look closer. Start to shake.

Navigating along this unpredictable river, I always knew my fragile little boat might take on water. I was prepared for that. I anticipated big cracks in the hull, in several places.

But I never pictured damage quite like this.

Next, I open the envelope and scan through each of the three certificates. One of them strikes me like a horsewhip.

The pain is searing.

My boat is sinking. And I'm going down with it.

19

Friday

Rootless

Could all this be a lie, too?

Could someone have falsified the documents, from within the administrative offices? There's definitely more than one lie in all this now . . . but that's still very unlikely.

What I've just read on these certificates is painfully clear.

The words are stark, harsh. Merciless.

My mother didn't die when I was a year old as my father's always said she did. She died the day I was born.

That's it then, the eye of the hurricane.

What I thought I knew about my life has just been struck off the map.

What happened that day?

What did you do, Dad?

Dad. Who was a doctor on 1 January 1976, that's what it says in black and white on the screenshot of my birth certificate. Dad who's never been a doctor. Dad who was so proud when I became the first doctor in the family.

My father, the stranger. Who's lied about everything, all along.

Has he lied about his feelings?

What am I to him really? A toy he can taunt and manipulate as he pleases? Maybe he regrets not abandoning me too . . .

Because this is what I can gather from reading these certificates: on 1 January 1976 my mother died in childbirth – and given the existence of Juliette, she died giving birth to twins. Though there is of course no record of Juliette in the documents. How appalling. What a terrible image.

Was my father there when it happened? Of course he was. He was a doctor at the time, he must have known all about it. I don't believe that a baby was stolen from the maternity unit. My father's told far too many lies to have nothing to hide.

The only remaining possibility is that, on that fateful day, my father decided in full consciousness to keep only one of us. Me.

My God.

Why, Dad? And how did you choose? Was Juliette not pretty enough? Did she cry too loudly, already so much more assertive than me? Or was it just chance? Did you throw a dice, toying with our lives by picking straws?

I'm disgusted by what I now know.

Whatever you say, it won't excuse what you did. Abandoning your daughter, Juliette. And holding your tongue.

For thirty-nine long years.

I think Désiré's asking me something but I'm not listening.

This is a nightmare. I'm going to wake up and everything will go back to normal. I close my eyes, then open them again. Désiré's looking at me, his face distraught. I'm here in real life or perhaps I'm in the fake one, the lie. But either way, it's mine.

My tears gradually turn to anger. Silent rage. My heart hardens. I get to my feet and throw up, right here, into a flowerbed in this park I so love. I hope you know this flowerbed, Dad. I hope you've nurtured it like all your secrets that I'm spewing all my loathing onto, on this July morning.

I was planning to see my father today, to force him to talk. I'm ready to confront him, readier than I've ever been.

Désiré tries to calm me, to soothe the fury rumbling inside me. He holds me back, tells me this might not be a good time to go and see my father, I should wait till my anger has subsided a little. I scream at him to go fuck himself, tell him I don't need him, I don't need anyone, and he's a burden, he's slowing me down. He wanted to be a safety valve, well, he's had what he came for. I immediately regret what I've said and apologize flatly but he's already walking away. I go after him, he doesn't turn around. I've driven him away. Him too. Like all the others.

I'm alone, yet again. I've always been alone, when it comes down to it. I always will be.

I'm in a terrible state when I get to my father's place.

I don't bother ringing the bell or knocking, I just go in and roar his name – a ball of screaming and anger. I search all round the apartment but have to accept the facts: he's not here. Everything's so tidy, it drives me insane. I need to break something, to disrupt this order. So I grab the gilded frame, the photo of the three of us together. A family that's too perfect to be real. I want to destroy the photo but I know I can't do it. I start crying again. I sit in my father's favourite armchair, the one just by the window, the one he used to sit in to read and to cry as he gazed at this very picture of the three of us, as it stood on the coffee table facing him. For a moment, I become him. The three of us look beautiful in the yellowing photo. We so deserved to be happy. It's all so heartbreaking: the lives, the deaths, the lies. I take the photo out of the frame and look at it more closely. I'm in my father's arms and my mother's standing near us, her expression slightly preoccupied. I've always thought she just wasn't looking at the camera. But the truth was very different.

I start to wonder where on earth my father can be. He's normally such a creature of habit. When he's in Paris, Friday mornings are devoted to his exercises, here in the living room. I open the fridge, just on the off-chance. Empty. Where is he? I need to see him, right here, right now. I ram the family photo – although just thinking those words makes me feel sick – into my handbag, take a big, deep breath, get up and walk out of the apartment without a backward glance.

Before leaving the building, I open his letter box and see that his mail has been taken, which means he can't be all that far away, or he hasn't been gone long. I need to see him, I can't not see him. I sit on a bench along the street and breathe into my little paper bag, hoping to steady my breathing and calm myself down before calling him. I mustn't let him hear the rank aggression that's taken hold of me.

When I feel ready, I call his mobile. Once, twice, three times. I leave a message on his voicemail, explaining calmly that my phone number has changed and letting him know how to get hold of me. I reiterate all this in a text.

Call me back, Dad, please call me back.

An hour later I still have no word from him.

I've decided to go back to my apartment, to pick up my bag and get to Marseilles as quickly as I can. To find Juliette.

I'm about to leave for the hospital when my phone rings at last. I throw myself at it, hoping it's my father.

It's not him.

It's far worse than that.

PART 3
Hours

20

Friday

Irreversible

The number on my screen is the pulmonology department at the Hôpital Nord – I've memorized it. I sit down before picking up, as a precaution. There's already been far too much emotion today and the fact that it's not Juliette herself calling but the hospital instantly makes my heartrate quicken. My back is bathed in a thin film of icy sweat.

It's a nurse. The one overseeing my sister's case.

Yes, I'm Laurence Delgrange.

The nurse asks me if I can get to the hospital as quickly as possible.

The ground gives way beneath my feet.

What's going on?

I can't be told anything over the phone. The head of department would like to see me.

'It'll take me four, maybe five hours to get to you, will that be OK?'

'Do your best, madame. Thank you and see you later. Good luck.'

Oh God, she's just wished me luck. What's happened? There aren't exactly thousands of different options.

I start to shake. My legs can't support me any more, I crumple to my knees on the floor of my apartment with the phone between my legs. And I stay there, motionless, staring blankly. For many minutes. I'm suffocating. I managed to reduce my use of paper bags at the beginning of the week, but they're back with a vengeance on this miserable afternoon.

I order a taxi and then catch a TGV without a reservation so I'm promptly reprimanded by a stubborn ticket inspector. I refuse to pay the fine and I'm within a hair's breadth of being frogmarched to a police desk when I burst into tears and my pitiful state neutralizes the man's hankering to see me incarcerated.

Next it's back into a taxi and views of Marseilles through tinted windows, with a driver flustered by this customer who sniffs all through the journey and uses up his whole supply of tissues. Then it's the hospital reception, the pulmonology department . . . and the waiting begins.

I don't actually have to wait long. A very engaging young woman with hair as red as Juliette's and mine – but a much prettier face – comes for me. I'm taken to a small, discreet room and immediately know what it's used for: the fact that I'm in this particular room isn't a good sign, I'm sure of that. Good news is communicated in corridors or on the ward. Two people come in and talk to me gently. I understand only too clearly what they tell me. No one asks me for proof of my identity, our likeness is so obvious.

As Juliette Delgrange's sister, I must be aware that her condition has taken a very sharp turn for the worse. Juliette is battling with an acute exacerbation of idiopathic pulmonary fibrosis.

Wait, what? The last I heard, cancer was suspected. Not fibrosis. There must be some mistake. They've definitely got this wrong.

'We suspected it might be cancer, amongst other possible illnesses, you're right. It's rare for fibrosis to present with such an acute exacerbation. But it does happen . . . and it has in Juliette's case. We're so very sorry, Madame Delgrange.'

My voice cracks as I ask them to stop telling me how sorry they are. They say they're sorry, then apologize again, using different words this time. I hold back the tide of tears threatening my eyes, my heart, my whole body, and in spite of everything I manage to formulate this question: why didn't they call me sooner?

'So long as the patient was in a fit state to do so, it was up to her to decide. We strenuously encouraged her to . . . but apparently she never did.'

Juliette was moved to resus this morning. I am listed as her first point of contact so the hospital called me as soon as the department's head consultant arrived.

My God. My God. My God. My God.

This is a fucking nightmare, a really real proper actual one, this time.

This is not good. Not good at all. I start to sob.

Juliette has idiopathic pulmonary fibrosis.

A terrible disease that affects the delicate tissue in the lungs. This usually supple flexible tissue allows each of us to make painless involuntary movements inside the ribcage. To breathe normally. In sufferers of this condition, these tissues gradually become fibrous and tough, and as this scarring spreads through both lungs, breathing becomes increasingly difficult.

Juliette's symptoms are exactly what you'd expect, the medics are right. But they could also apply to plenty of other complaints . . . are they sure of their diagnosis? They can't be 100 per cent sure, medicine isn't infallible. But all other possible conditions have been eliminated over the last few days.

This illness is an absolute bitch. A bitch with an unknown cause – which is what 'idiopathic' means. It's rare, for sure, but still affects nearly one hundred thousand people in Europe.

An illness with an unpronounceable name.

But crucially, most crucially, an incurable illness.

To date there is no effective treatment for it. The fibrous tissue never returns to normal. The lesions are irreversible. The prognosis is grim. Half of sufferers die within three years. I know all this because I came face to face with the condition six years ago: one of my patients had it. And died of it.

The air is becoming unbreathable. I'm panting now, faster and faster. I need to calm down but just can't. My sobbing unleashes the worst paroxysm of hyperventilation that my body has ever had to withstand. I think I can see the doctors panicking and rushing around but I can't be sure, everything's going hazy.

My brain needs air or I'll be done for too.

It needs to look after itself, to go on pause to reoxygenate itself.

I'm going to pass out, I know I am.

Right now.

*

When I come round I'm lying on a hospital bed.

I gradually acknowledge everything they told me, but I've stopped crying. My complete breakdown seems to have dried up my tears.

I think about Marie, Paola, Gabriel, Raphaël, all the people who love Juliette and have no idea anything's going on. All the people I will have to tell the news to, when they don't even know me. It's up to me to bring this suffering into their lives. Juliette has treated me unfairly. She should have talked to them when the time was right. She's shirked her responsibility. And dumped it onto me. I've done nothing to deserve this. Nothing but love my sister. For a few days.

Just for a moment I think to myself that, at the end of the day, it would have been better if I'd never known Juliette. If you don't know you love someone, you're protected from pain. Living in ignorance to avoid going under. I shake my head to dispel this line of thought. It's pointless and unhealthy. And wrong. So wrong. I know that if I were given the choice, I'd rather die than never have met my sister.

Oh, Juliette, it may have been only a few days but I'm so happy I met you! I'm so happy I loved you!

When I'm up on my feet, I'm told I can go to see my sister, although she won't be able to reply. They're not even sure she can hear. I hesitate for a long time, but in the end I don't go. I can't. I don't want to see her like that. I'd rather cling to the lovely memories I have of Sunday and Monday. They seem so long ago but also so recent.

On the way back to Avignon I feel as if my brain is empty, made of cotton wool. It's preparing to deal with the worst. That nurse wished me good luck, and I'm going to need it.

*

It's gone eleven in the evening when I finally walk into Juliette's apartment. I pour myself a glass of wine – it's the first time in my life that I've had an alcoholic drink on my own; there's a first time for everything.

I try to look at things rationally: yes, Juliette could die. But she could live, too.

There *is* a way out. A glimmer of hope. Just one. A pulmonary transplant.

A glimmer of hope that relies on other people being brain-dead; what a painful irony. A glimmer of hope full of uncertainty because there aren't enough available lungs. And if any of them are deemed transplantable, they may not be morphologically or genetically compatible with the patient in most urgent need. Dying on the waiting list for donor organs, or during surgery or when transplanted organs are rejected . . . these are all grisly realities.

The medical team have put Juliette on the list of 'super-urgent' cases waiting for pulmonary transplants. I'm familiar with this official term, and I've always thought it lent a note of cosmic combat to this most dramatic of situations. I've always thought it would soothe families, probably reassuring them about how well their loved one's situation was being handled. Now, to my great distress, I realize that's not how it feels at all.

In a flash I sit bolt upright. A word reverberates inside my head.

A word that could change everything.

Sitting here in Juliette's living room with my phone in my hand, I open a search engine, click on a page, then another, enter my username and password. I'm shaking. I'm hoping . . .

I jump in surprise, splutter a curse that's at least fifty years out of date.

A green icon is flashing.

My whole body strains towards the screen.

They've come through a little sooner than anticipated, but it's the middle of the summer, there was probably less demand.

The results are available.

A simple document appears. Our lives reduced to a few lines. Juliette is my twin, my father is our father. It's confirmed in black and white.

My eyes go cloudy. Then overflow.

The solution is right here in front of me.

Summarized in just one word: genetic.

The one and only adult who is absolutely bound to be genetically compatible with Juliette is me. Her twin.

Clearly I'm not brain-dead. But I hold my sister's life in my hands.

21

Friday

Life or death

I could give Juliette back the world that's been stolen from her.

I could give my life for her.

I could save her.

Juliette wanted me to take her place in her life. The truth is, I could take her place in death. Yes, me, the one who's lived with our real father all these years.

Is it really possible? There's a chance I could sacrifice myself and some technical or ethical problem might get in the way of the plan. Then we'd both die and it would all have been for nothing.

Think, Romane, think.

I'm familiar with the organ transplant process, I've followed it from waiting list to convalescence with three of my patients. I go onto the bio-med agency site to check that my knowledge of the field is still up to date – and it is.

In order for my organ donation to be acknowledged, there must be absolutely no doubt about my suicide. If not, a murder investigation could be opened, wasting precious time. So I need to leave a completely unambiguous letter and make sure witnesses see me alone just before I do the deed. I also need to make sure there's no detectable family connection between Juliette and me. Organ donations are anonymous in France. Donor and recipient families never know each other's identities. My sacrifice would struggle to clear the hurdles of ethical committees if it were established that Juliette is my sister. As far as the hospital is concerned, Juliette's sister is called Laurence Delgrange, the name Juliette invented when she named me as her first point of contact. As far as the authorities are concerned, she's an only child.

When my body is found, I'll have my donor card and my ID card in my pocket. The big-nosed black-haired teenager in my collector's item of a 1992 ID card looks nothing like the Juliette Delgrange of today. Given my lifestyle, any other research into me will, of course, prove fruitless – I have no passport, no more recent ID, no Internet presence.

On the other hand, my face will have to be unrecognizable. I'll make sure of that. It won't be a problem. My father, who's always been afraid I'll be assaulted, gave me a handgun and a course of shooting lessons five years ago. His paranoia will finally come in useful, in the last moments of my life.

First thing tomorrow I'll go back to Paris to get the gun from my apartment.

That night I'll take a hotel room very close to the Hôpital Nord. I'll call the emergency services, wait a few minutes and when I hear the paramedics in the corridor, I'll end my life. Efficiently. I know exactly how to do it to keep my lungs intact. And give them to Juliette.

So the paramedics will find a woman completely unrelated to Juliette Delgrange but a perfect histological match for her (the tests will reveal only our compatibility, not the fact that we're twins). What's more, a woman with first-rate lungs: I've never smoked in my life and my hyperventilating is totally psychological – every test under the sun has proved that. A woman of the same body size who died less than a kilometre from the Hôpital Nord. What a stroke of luck for the patient on the 'super-urgent' list.

Of course, the transplant might not take, but with lungs identical to the recipient's I'm sure there's a very low risk of rejection. Juliette will have every chance of pulling through. She'll be able to carry on with her life, with her loved ones. Marie will be happy, Paola and Gabriel will be happy . . .

I may not have achieved much in my life, but I still have the ability to achieve something meaningful with my death.

I can make it beautiful, generous, purposeful.
My father will lose one daughter, but gain another.
A much better one.
Better adapted to happiness.
Really?

THAT CHILDHOOD

It's difficult being a father. Difficult raising a child on your own.

I did my best, Romane.

From the moment you were born, I've had only one fear: that something would happen to you. That you would die. That you too would abandon me. So I did everything I could to minimize the risks.

First, by removing your twin from the equation. And then by protecting you at all costs.

I do realize that in my case it went beyond normal precautions. I fretted about you sleeping alone, about you walking, trying things out for yourself. I always found it incredibly difficult leaving you with other people to look after you. We can only count on ourselves in this life, I learned that the hard way.

The hospital meant a life of shifts and regular night duty. How could I leave you to sleep when I was at work far away? I had abandoned Marie, your mother, on that first day of 1976, and that failing on my part had proved fatal. I couldn't come to terms with being away from you for a single night. I was the best person to protect you. The only person. The person who wanted your happiness above anything else, who put you before everything, certainly before his own life.

So that I could keep a closer eye on you I first considered going independent, setting up my own practice. But whatever I did, I was haunted by images of Marie on that freezing bed. The sight of a bandage, of blood was enough to make me weak at the knees. I thought the problem would pass but it made my day-to-day life impossible. On 1 January the following year I decided to make a break once and for all, to change my life and career. I chose a calm job, far removed from cries of pain, and one that allowed me the time to bring you up. And love you. I thought I'd be there a few months, but I ended up tending Buttes-Chaumont park for thirty-five happy years. I loved that life. Of course, my salary wasn't what it had been, but what I gained in serenity, in being able to breathe and being free to care for you, my darling – that was beyond priceless.

We moved house, coming to the more working-class neighbourhood near my work. I decided to change everything, to put new happiness into our lives and our story. I made the decision never to tell you about the past. To spare you the wounds of my own childhood. And the wounds of my adult life. I no longer had it in me to tell anyone what really happened the day you were born. I didn't have it in me to describe what I did when I lost the woman I loved beyond reason. Juliette's screaming face wrapped in the blanket haunted me every evening before I went to sleep and the way I'd abandoned her ate away at me steadily. I didn't have it in me to go through it all again, even just in words. It would have stirred up far too much pain.

I wanted you to have an image of Marie as the sunny person she really was. And for you to know she loved you more than anything. I wanted her to stay alive in my heart and yours. Sadly, her death was the one fact I could never change, even if I wanted to cut it out of our lives. So I reinvented your mother's death. I imagined a year lived with her. A year as a family of three, complete with a lovely photograph, anecdotes, happy memories. Then I invented a family outing, a day on which she made a luminously brave sacrifice. I wanted to make Marie the heroine she deserved to be, ready to risk everything out of love for you, her daughter. No screams, no tears, no suffering. Just a heroic death, a brief impact. Definitive, almost beautiful. To save you.

It tore me in two when you first went to school. I had no choice, obviously. You were growing, I had to let you develop, let you have your childhood. I would count the hours till it was time to pick you up. What some people call 'mummy time'. What a cruel misnomer for children who don't have a mother. And oh, the anxiety for me, all through the day when I couldn't be watching over you.

I had to teach you to harden yourself, immunize yourself. A level-headed child is worth a hundred thousand who aren't. I told you the worst atrocities that could happen to a little girl, a teenager, and an adult woman. So that you'd be careful, you'd build yourself a strong carapace, you'd consider the consequences of your actions before you did anything. I passed on all my fears to you, I realize that. I couldn't help it. I needed to make you invincible, untouchable. I passed on a fierce determination to defend yourself, and the best ways to achieve that, in any situation. But, right from your earliest years, I also fuelled the things that now hold you back. The sort of paranoia that at the time seemed appropriate, necessary.

The whole episode when you broke your ankle in 1985 played a key role in your future career. When your teacher called me, I experienced the most indescribable distress. When I heard her voice on the phone, I thought she was going to tell me you'd died. That phone call revived the pain of loss, and the agony ruptured all the stitches over the mutilations of my past. I soon realized your injury wasn't very serious, but I felt overwhelmed. I knew I couldn't watch over you twenty-four hours a day, you would become increasingly independent and I couldn't keep you in a cage forever.

It was then that I decided you would become a doctor. The profession I could no longer exercise would be yours.

I had to be sure you knew your body in minute detail so you could identify the tiniest malfunction, know what treatment you needed, know how to save yourself, when the time came. I'm sure you remember this, I immediately started playing the game Operation with you, giving you videos of Once Upon a Time . . . Life *and books about the human body. I wanted you to think of medicine as fun, appealing. By the time you were twelve you cheerfully announced you were going to be a GP. I was proud, satisfied. Relieved.*

As for everything else – public transport, accidents in the home and nutcases of every type – all I could do was instil in you a keen awareness of danger. So I did. And for a long time I thought I'd succeeded. I now see that, by passing on my fears, I nurtured your hypochondria and anxieties. But I can't change the past.

You're alive now, you're beautiful, gorgeous – seeing you every day fills me with happiness.

I love you, Romane. More than anything.

22

Saturday

Three, two, one

As I piece together my morbid suicide scenario, the heat of the moment almost makes me forget what this is all about.

Running towards the edge of the precipice, not stopping, not looking to the left or right, and saving Juliette. Carefully shut away behind huge blinkers.

That's the theory.

In practice, I've been paralysed by the hyperventilating of a panic attack for several minutes now.

This is my death I'm contemplating; I can't behave as if a decision like this was just a question of reason. Feelings will gain the upper hand at the end of the day. And whatever they urge me to do will be unbearable because one of us will die.

Which of our two lives is worth more?

How can I establish any sort of priority without exploring the darkest hours of our lives, without prying into terrifying and despicable details?

Am I really prepared to sacrifice myself for this sister whose very existence I discovered only a few days ago?

A few incredibly intense days. A few days that have turned all my assumptions on their head and have profoundly changed me.

A few days in which I've found myself contemplating a relationship with a man – even though I then drove him away, but still . . . for the first time in forever I've projected myself into the future. I've laughed and cried as never before. I've felt so alive. What a sadistic twist of fate to find death knocking at my door today.

Would Juliette be happier than me? Yes, most likely. Juliette doesn't need to learn happiness, she already has it in her, she's a veteran of happiness, while I'm just a beginner. And anyway, Juliette has a daughter. I can't take the child's mother away from her.

Yes, but the thing is, the truth is right here in my guts.

It's irrational and powerful, carved indelibly into my flesh.

I want to live.

I want to fall in love, have a child, overcome my fears, travel, breathe, sing, laugh, cry, gasp, savour, fall, get up again, feel myself existing. I want to live for all of that. And for much more too. I wouldn't have been able to formulate it this clearly a few days ago, but today it's all so obvious.

I want to live and I'm prepared to shout it from the

rooftops – yes, me, who's normally so discreet, tiptoeing through my own life.

But how could I survive Juliette's death?

I've lived thirty-nine years without her but I'm terrified at the thought of losing her. It may seem absurd that I've come to love her so dearly in such a short space of time. Is that because Juliette is now the only person I can trust? The only one who's never lied to me? And can I actually be sure she's never lied to me? I don't know, I can't know, but I cling to the thought that she's been honest with me.

We cling to whatever we can when everything falls apart.

All at once, right in the middle of this swirling chaos, I glimpse something else.

A possibility. A flash of light ripping through the dark sky.

A crazy idea. The craziest I've ever had.

But the best and most beautiful too.

I can feel an adrenaline rush. All my senses are alert. I turn on Juliette's laptop.

Could it be? Is it possible?

The further I get with my research, the harder my heart beats. It's almost coming out of my chest.

Yes, this has been tried before. It's been done. It has worked for several dozen patients around the world. It's exceptional but it has been done. In France? Yes, in France too.

I check again. As if I could have been wrong . . . I'm a doctor but I've never heard of this before. It looks as if there are other doctors out there who are even crazier than I am. My God, it really has been done. It even has a name.

Live donor lung transplant.

One lung each to save three lives.

Or rather a pulmonary lobe each.

We all have five pulmonary lobes: three on the right and two on the left. Live donor lung transplants involve taking one lobe from each compatible donor and transplanting them into the recipient's body. The human animal is remarkable, capable of living without one of its pulmonary lobes. There is a risk of mortality for donors – there always is – but it's very low. And there are usually only minimal after-effects.

My father's still young, strong enough to undergo this sort of operation, and is a model of clean living: his lungs are as healthy as mine. I can't be sure that he's absolutely compatible with Juliette – a parent isn't necessarily – but there's a very high chance because the DNA tests have confirmed what I already knew: he definitely is Juliette's father as well as mine.

There's hope.

I start laughing out loud, sitting here alone in this apartment in Avignon, late in the night.

I laugh at this explosion of life amid the desolation.

I laugh with fear. With joy. With pride. With distress. With happiness.

I laugh about the extraordinary ordeal I'm preparing to confront.

I laugh because I'm happy, right now.

Happy to have an opportunity to bring the three of us together: Juliette, my father and myself.

Happy to give my father a chance to atone. It won't replace the thirty-nine lost years, but could radically change the thirty-nine to come.

Would this sort of transplant be possible in a 'super-urgent' case? I haven't a sodding clue but it's worth trying. It's worth talking to the medical team and trying to persuade them. And quickly.

If I'm going to do that, I'll need to have my father with me, obviously.

I need to find him. To tell him I now know everything. What he did is unforgivable but there is a road to redemption. Dad, you can offer your second daughter a second life. It will be such a wonderful gesture that I'll find it in me to forgive you – I'm sure of that. And Juliette will forgive you in turn. Her family will thank you, will thank us. This ordeal will make us stronger, individually and together.

I call my father again. It's two in the morning.

Still no reply. *Pick up, Dad, please pick up.*

A second attempt. A third. A fourth.

I'll call millions of times if that's what it takes.

A click. A groggy, anxious voice.

'Romane? What's . . . nothing's happened to you, has it? What are you calling for at this time of night?'

It turns out he hasn't received my messages, his phone was stolen two days ago, 'Who'd have thought it could happen in the back of beyond like that!' He's been away for a few days in the Auvergne, in Saint-Paul-de-Salers. He needed some fresh air after my visit on Sunday, which . . . disturbed him. He apologizes again for hitting me. He doesn't know what came over him. He's so terribly sorry, and hopes I'll forgive him.

Right now I want to forgive him for everything. If only he agrees to what I'm about to suggest. But I can't tell him all this over the phone.

'Where are you at the moment? Still in the Auvergne?'

'No, I'm in Montpellier. I've stopped off before the next leg of my journey in the south-west. Romane . . . would you mind . . . would you be able to join me? It would make me so happy if you agreed to spend a few days' holiday with me . . . don't you think the time has come for us to see a bit more of each other?'

You have no idea how much I'd like to join you, and how much more we'll see of each other in the next few weeks, Dad.

It occurs to me that if I go to Montpellier, we'll lose precious hours. It would be far more expedient for us to meet in Marseilles. So I decide that's where we'll rendezvous.

'I'm on holiday too, actually . . . I've got a whole programme of things in Provence. You know what I'm like, always very organized.'

I can hear his smile on the phone.

'I'd love it if you could join me in Marseilles, Dad.'

'Are you serious, darling? You in Marseilles . . . does that mean you've taken a train? That's revolutionary, Romane . . . and wonderful, too. It means you've managed to overcome your fear of public transport. I'm . . . I'm proud of you, Romane.'

He's moved, I can hear it in his voice. Ridiculous though this is, it makes me want to cry.

'I'd be delighted to join you, darling,' he continues. 'I haven't really booked anything for the rest of my trip, so . . . I'll hop on a train in the morning, if you don't mind letting me sleep for a few hours.'

He laughs lightly.

I've missed his laugh, I suddenly realize. The laugh that accompanied my childhood games, all those high-speed chases around the apartment that invariably ended in tickling fights; the laugh that exploded if I plunged my nose a little too deeply into his incomparable pasta with vegetables (his ultimate speciality); the laugh that has punctuated all the major stepping stones of my life. The laugh that has always been such a blessing for me.

We arrange to meet.

'I'll see you tomorrow at about one, on the forecourt of Saint-Charles station.'

'I'll be there.'

'Goodnight, Dad.'

'Goodnight, my darling.'

A moment's hesitation, at both ends.

'I love you, Romane.'

'I love you too, Dad.'

He hangs up. I dissolve into tears and smile at the same time. I think it must be like having a rainbow on my face, but I know it's probably more a case of hideous streams of mascara.

Who cares? I now feel absolutely sure we're going to save Juliette.

23

Saturday
If you knew

Saturday morning. The sun has come out again over Avignon. As if I'm now in charge of everything, including the weather. At midday a taxi will come to take me to Marseilles. To my father, to Juliette.

I'll need to be strong. I must talk to my father as gently as possible, and I mustn't judge him, not now. What matters now – urgently – is Juliette. I need to stay focused on my aim: persuading him to donate a pulmonary lobe to Juliette. Whatever happens, I mustn't antagonize him by asking him to justify the unjustifiable. The truth can come later.

I think we'll succeed, and that my father will also be compatible. And Juliette will live. We'll all live. I think so, but I'm aware of the risks. In Juliette's case they're huge. I know she's far from in the clear. I know she could die, with or without the transplants. For my father and myself the risk of dying is virtually negligible. But it's all in that *negligible*. I don't trust *negligible*. There was a *negligible* chance that the stranger spotted by Madame Lebrun was my twin sister. But then . . . I don't want to know whether Juliette will still be alive tomorrow. I can't be sure I will be myself after this far from routine operation. I hope so with all my heart but the truth is, I have no idea.

Over the course of the night, torn between pain and hope, I wrote two letters and hid them in Juliette's bedside table because they're intended to be read only if there's a dramatic outcome.

The first is for Paola and Gabriel, and it tells them everything that I know: their compromise with the truth, and my father's, my pact with Juliette and my wanting to break this cycle of lies. I'd like Marie to know all about her mother's family background, which is also my family background, and Marie's too. I know the pain of growing up with niggling doubt and suspicions. I know the terror of never being fully in focus, never having a face to identify with your roots. I don't want that for my niece.

And so my second letter is for Marie, and it explains why her mother kept quiet about her illness, in order to spare all of them, in order to spare her. My letter tells her that her mother loved her, she told me so dozens of times in the space of a few hours, and she will always be with her. I tell her that her mother knows she's strong, beautiful and intelligent. Destined for an amazing life. It's the letter I wish I'd had from my own mother. Perhaps it would have given me the resources, the confidence I needed to make my way through life more serenely. I feel that a letter full of love like this can't fail to build the wonderful woman that Marie will grow into. The letter also tells her what's about to happen now: one last morning spent not with her mother, but with me. Her aunt. Who hardly knows her but to whom she already means so much.

I call Paola first thing and ask if she could bring Marie to the bookshop this morning because I want to hug her, I want to hug both of them.

'Is something wrong, my weasel?'

'No, Mum, just a mother who loves her daughter.'

'What a beautiful thing to say, *tesoro*. Of course we'll come and see you. Not for long because I want to get to the supermarket before all the tourists turn up.'

'No problem, Mum.'

'Tell me . . . could I have Marie until Raphaël gets back? I promised I'd make a panettone for her and I haven't had time yet, so I just wondered . . .'

'No problem, Mum.'

Given my plans for the next few days, that's what I was hoping. Paola just beat me to it.

I open the shop at 9.30 and five minutes later Paola comes in with Marie, who throws her arms around me. I'm astonished to see her dressed entirely in blue and she explains that pink week is over because her YouTube guru says it's all about blue now. Far more difficult to achieve with food so white is also acceptable. Thanks for that concession, YouTube.

Paola comes up to me.

'Your eyes look puffy, a bit red too. Have you been crying?'

'Not at all, Mum. Maybe I've got conjunctivitis brewing. I'll wait a couple of days and see if I get over it by the end of the weekend . . .'

She smiles.

'If you want to go for a little walk with Marie, I can stay here for half an hour. I love helping in the bookshop, you meet such lovely people here . . . By the way, how's that charming Désiré of yours?'

'That's nothing to do with you, Mum . . . and he's not *my* Désiré . . .'

'Whatever you say . . . he was *molto bello*, anyway. You have very good taste . . . you must get that from me . . . I mean, it's only your looks that are like your father, everything else is from me!'

Paola laughs heartily, kisses me and plants a noisy kiss on Marie's cheek. Does Paola believe what she's saying, telling her daughter that she *really* looks like her father? Has she buried the adoption somewhere deep inside her, has she managed to convince herself of another version of reality? I'm sure she has. With passing time, the impossible has become the truth: they are

Juliette's real parents. In their guts, in their hearts, in their day-to-day lives for thirty-nine years. There's no other explanation.

*

I take Marie into the centre of Avignon, to the huge square, the Place de l'Horloge, which is already alive with the hubbub of hundreds of voices. We choose a table outside an ice-cream parlour, where we're probably the first customers of the day. The dazzling chemical blue of 'Smurf's Delight' flavour irresistibly appeals to Marie. She insists on taking a photo to 'show Daddy how good we're being with blue food'. I was thinking of settling for a sensible chocolate cornet but end up throwing myself into the Smurf ice-cream adventure too.

We sit there for a moment before Marie offers to show me more 'work' from her favourite YouTuber. I'm happy to accept, and I marvel at how adeptly she handles the phone. She can't yet read but she navigates with voice commands . . . which I myself have no idea how to use. This generation weaned on apps is scary. The YouTube channel presenter is scary too: she must be twenty-five but behaves like a twelve-year-old. Is she playing a part or is she really like that? I tend to believe it's the latter, which makes me think the world's gone mad.

Marie can't stop saying how 'super-happy' she is with her blue ice cream and our impromptu YouTube viewing session, and she seems to mean it. Her glowing face can't be lying.

We head back to the bookshop and I spin out our walk, extending my time with her, and making the most of her sudden tiredness to carry her in my arms. I hug her to me, good and close. I can't tear myself away. But I shall have to. I give her a long, slow kiss on her forehead and whisper, 'Goodbye, my little weasel who I love.' I manage not to cry. She hugs me back, but not for long. She doesn't know that she needs to squeeze me tight, as tight as she can, that the sensation of this last moment is actually crucial. So I suggest we compete to see who can squeeze harder. She giggles as she crushes my jaw and smothers me with kisses, and I kiss her back with a heavy heart while my tears teeter behind a fragile sea wall.

I watch as Paola carries off the little blue-and-blonde bundle. I'm proud of myself. I'm proud of what I'm about to do. I don't know if I've been proud of myself before, ever. Even with what I did with my career. It's high time I was. I stand there like that till the bookshop door closes behind them.

I wait a few minutes to be sure Paola and Marie have gone, then I let my tears flow. I held them back, just on the edge, until now. But I can't hold them any longer.

I'm starting to see all the things that have passed me by in life. In some instances out of laziness. Mostly out of fear. I've lived my whole life in fear. Fear of everything, all the time. Even though there was no threat hovering over me. I censored myself, barricaded myself behind paper screens, constantly dulling my own existence. It's ridiculous really but it's only now that I realize my fear of dying has stopped me living. In any event, I'm glad of those few moments with Marie. A little extra. An interlude full of sunlight.

*

Just as I'm about to close the shop for an indeterminate period, the bell rings and I hear a familiar voice.

'You're a very unusual woman, Romane.'

Désiré is standing in the doorway. Smiling. Holding a small – and obviously homemade – bunch of flowers. I remember what I said to him yesterday morning, an eternity ago.

'Désiré, I'm so sorry. Honestly, I didn't mean to–'

'I know, Romane,' he interrupts.

I look at him. I want to take him in my arms, right here, right now. To kiss him wildly. And more, let's be honest. I'm not afraid this morning.

He hands me the pretty flowers.

'They have various names, including four o'clock flower and *belle-de-nuit* because they reveal their beauty at nightfall and close again at dawn. I thought they suited us rather well. These modest flowers are an invitation to further nocturnal outings. I know a particularly nice bridge . . . but I do have other resources too.'

I could try anything, I'd *like* to try anything with him. I desperately want to. But I don't want to cause him pain. He can't possibly guess . . . I don't know what state I'll be in when I wake from my donor operation. I risk a metaphor about short-lived butterflies, make a mess of it, hear myself laughing stupidly – I'm suddenly a fifteen-year-old. Désiré must be fed up with listening to my inane remarks because he comes up to me and puts a finger on my lips. The touch of him paralyses me. The warmth of him electrifies me.

He leans his face towards me. I can feel his breathing, smell his minty breath. It's years since I've experienced this. Have I ever actually experienced it? Désiré kisses me. Slowly. Keeps moving closer. How could he get any closer? But he can. His hands become firmer. I surrender. It's a soft, moist, voluptuous feeling. Our kiss tastes like minty popcorn – a combination that makes me smile. He notices and slightly relaxes his hold . . . enough for a moment of lucidity to flash across my feeble mind. I can't. I mustn't go any further. It's a slippery slope. It's dangerous. The feelings that are surfacing inside me are the sort that could erode my willpower and destroy my determination to see things through to the end. And risk my life for Juliette. I can't possibly start anything new only hours before the deadline.

I gently extricate myself from Désiré's embrace. Tell him I need time. That he's terribly attractive but I can't go any further this morning. He smiles, tells me he understands. And I have his number. And there are other types of flower, ones that come alive during the day and are just as beautiful. And it definitely was a good thing that he was drawn to this bookshop that day a little while ago when there was a reception going on in here. And he'll wait to hear from me. I bite the inside of my cheek, hesitate, then give him one last, furtive kiss. A stolen kiss. My first. Perhaps also my last.

*

It's 11.50. The morning is almost over.

I book one final taxi. Avignon to Marseilles. At least a hundred euros. The journey of my life, taking me to my sister's life. I don't haggle about the fare.

It will be here within fifteen minutes.

*

I sit on a chair in the kitchen but can't keep still. I don't know why but seeing Désiré has stirred up the feeling that settled in my stomach, the feeling that I've missed *something*.

It's back. It's getting stronger. I'm so close to the goal.

What did he say that day on the bridge, what the flip did he say?

What did he say *today*?

I go back over how I felt at the time. What he did and said.

And all at once it's obvious.

The reception. Désiré mentioned a reception at the bookshop.

The champagne that lured him in when he was first in Avignon, he told me about it on the bridge. And mentioned it again a few minutes ago.

When I was on Juliette's computer the other evening, I saw photos of various events she'd organized at the bookshop. That's when I first had this feeling. And every mention of the reception has reawakened it. I saw *something* in amongst those photos. *Something* I haven't been able to shake off since.

I throw myself at the computer, snap it open feverishly. I've got ten minutes before the taxi arrives. I concentrate on the file of photos with the straightforward name 'Author events'.

My fear mounts as I scroll through the images.

One, two, three, four photos, no, no, no, no.

Five, six, seven, eight. There it is.

My body stiffens and my blood freezes as my eyes become transfixed.

It's not possible. How could I have missed this the other evening?

My father. My father in Juliette's photos. My father in the crowd at an author's signing at the bookshop. Taken less than a month ago.

I can feel tears welling. I zoom in, study the figure more closely. It really is him, I'm absolutely sure of it. I continue with my research and my tears start to flow. My father appears in other photos. Worse than that, in one picture he's smiling, clutching a glass of champagne that he's sharing with Juliette.

My head's reeling, I can't breathe.

I keep telling myself it's not possible. I need to lie down.

Everything's falling apart. I can't be sure of anything any more.

I keep saying the same words over and over again.

Words whose full implications I don't yet understand.

Juliette and my father know each other.

THAT DAUGHTER

When exactly did it start?

It's difficult to date the phenomenon because it now feels as if this insidious, unspeakable pain has always been there. Something corrosive rooted inside my body. A blade, a sharp scalpel diving into my still-fresh wounds. Sustaining the stomach ulcer that you've never known was there, Romane. I've always thought it was a trifling thing, a minor punishment compared to the enormity of the wrong I committed.

For decades now this thing commonly known as remorse has gnawed at me, devoured me.

For decades I've known I pulverized part of my life, part of yours. And part of hers.

Juliette. My other daughter. Your sister.

When you blew out twenty candles, something inside me stirred. Of course, the wrong had been done. And I had decided to do it. Whatever I did now, I couldn't change anything about it. Ever. But I needed to know what had happened to Juliette. Whether she was happy. I had an intuition – a hope – that she was. Or was that one way of letting myself off the hook, of appeasing my pain? I needed to know for sure. If I left it, it would be too late.

At twenty, she still had her life ahead of her.

At twenty, I could still make a difference in her life.

I hired a private detective, like in a B-movie. Less glamorous, more caffeine-dependent, built more like a bear than a Hollywood star. But frighteningly effective. A few contacts in the relevant administrative circles, a significant sum of money, and I was given Juliette's name and address. That was in March 1996.

The day I learned that she still had the name I'd hastily scribbled down on that boundlessly heartbreaking day, the name your mother had chosen, I was overwhelmed with emotion. Not only was Juliette alive, she was still Juliette. When I was handed a clandestinely snapped photograph of the young woman she'd grown into, my body literally started to bleed. Juliette was so like you. The day you were born I didn't give any thought to the fact that you were identical twins, but that photograph really brought it home to me. I had to spend a few days in hospital having the ulcer treated, and managed to hide this from you: you were in your third year of medicine, you had other things on your mind. You thought it was a good idea for me to grant myself a proper break at last.

It was another few weeks before I made up my mind. I'd come up with the ambitious idea of involving myself in Juliette's life. One way or another. I didn't want to be intrusive. The detective had informed me that Juliette appeared to be happy and perfectly healthy. So young but already sure of where she was going. She worked in a bookshop in Avignon, where her family now lived. Her family. Not us. Not me. Those words have always pained me. And I only have myself to blame.

It wasn't until thirteen years later that she opened A Word from Juliette. I encouraged her to, and then helped her. I'll come to that.

In May 1996 – I'll never forget it – I rallied all my strength and decided to meet her. To form a connection with her. Having failed to be a father, I hoped to become a friend. Before even speaking to her, I'd set myself clear limits about my intervention. If what the detective had told me was true, if Juliette was happy with her adoptive family, there was no question of sabotaging her happiness. The time had come for reparation, but softly-softly. I must respect her life, participate cautiously, discreetly. I would never reveal my true identity. Lying once more. Lying again and forever. In the end, my life is all lies. But it's the life I have.

One morning I turned up at the bookshop where Juliette worked and wandered around the shelves, not daring to look at her. I knew she was there, I'd seen her red head bent over a display unit. After a few minutes she'd finished what she was doing and came over to ask what she could do to help me. I looked her right in the eye and felt my tears welling. I wanted to say, 'Everything,' but simply replied, 'Nothing, thank you. I'm just looking.' She nodded, smiled and added automatically that if I needed her, she'd be right there. I let her walk away, turned around, my face ravaged with emotion, and mumbled, 'Me too.'

After that I took to having a few days off every month. I told you a different version, Romane, but I spent those days in Avignon.

I became a regular customer at the bookshop. I gave my name as 'Monsieur Joseph', and started having literary conversations with Juliette. My daughter. And now my official bookseller. She recommended books with that infectious enthusiasm, joy and verve of hers; I would read them and then we'd discuss them on my return a few weeks later. Our conversations grew longer. I'd identified the quiet days, days when Juliette could spend more time with a loyal customer. Those few hours spent with her were magical. And I'm not afraid to admit it.

I met her adoptive parents at the bookshop. Paola's exuberance frightened me at first. In some ways she reminded me of my own mother. But I could soon see the unconditional love between them. As for her father, Gabriel, Juliette would mention him sometimes and her face would light up with a smile. I played along, of course, but with a heavy heart. The day that I saw Juliette and her father together my heart broke. It hurt me to see this family living their life. I wondered which of you had had the better deal at the end of the day. By abandoning Juliette, I'd offered her the possibility of living in a real home. By keeping you with me, Romane, I'd condemned you to my fears, and exposed you to my obscure atonements for my most abject wrongs. I'm not blind. I very soon realized that of my two daughters, Juliette was the one who was flourishing. And that was nothing to do with me.

In any event, I'm infinitely grateful to that couple for taking in Juliette, for raising her so well and giving her so much love. She deserved it.

I've loathed myself all these years. I wanted to right the wrong. Ease my conscience. But it can never really be eased.

I've never been able to give the correct dose of love, I realize that now. All I ever wanted, Romane, was to show you how much I loved you. I didn't mean to smother you. But it was the only way I knew how.

The only thing I could expect from Juliette was this kindly salesgirl-customer relationship. And I could work in the shadows to improve her day-to-day life, like a guardian angel.

I had an opportunity to do just that when I could tell that Juliette was starting to feel unfulfilled at the bookshop where she worked. It was 2009, crowdfunding was just becoming a recognized finance system. I encouraged her to look into it, to set up a fund to finance the beginnings of her own independent bookshop. She did it. Three hundred anonymous contributors supported her project. It was amazing. Juliette was thrilled. She thanked me again and again for giving her such a wonderful idea. Our friendship grew closer. Or even . . . special.

Of those three hundred contributors, there were some two hundred she didn't know. Pseudonyms, payments. Of course, I was those two hundred people. I took out two loans from two different banks, and all my savings went into it as well. But I was so happy to be contributing, even modestly, to Juliette's well-being. It seemed so little.

That same year, Juliette discovered she was pregnant, and I felt I could try something more significant. I wanted this child, my first – and so far only – granddaughter to belong symbolically in our family. Juliette had outlandish ideas for names. Complicated, 'fashionable' names. I'm sure our conversations brought her round to more classic options. At quite an early stage I introduced your mother's name into the mix. She immediately thought it charming. From then on I increased the frequency of my visits and was quick to refer to the unborn child as 'Marie'. Which made your sister laugh and say something like, 'Steady on now, Monsieur Joseph . . .' When Juliette laughs, and when you laugh, Romane, I see Marie, your mother. Your laughs, yours and hers, break my heart and mend it all at the same time.

The idea worked its way through, but even so, right up to the last minute I didn't know what she would choose. And I didn't know Raphaël so I had no traction with him.

When the baby was born, Juliette sent me a simple text.

Marie was born this morning. Thank you, Monsieur Joseph.

It was one of the best days of my life.

24

Saturday

So be it

It's three minutes past twelve. I can see the taxi waiting opposite.

I'm completely lost.

Is everyone manipulating me? What for? I try to separate the truth from the lies but don't get anywhere.

I don't understand any of it.

But I do need to leave because two things are absolutely clear: Juliette *is* my sister (DNA doesn't lie) and she's going to die if she doesn't have a transplant in the next few days (the staff of a major hospital would never play-act on such a serious subject, this isn't *The Truman Show*). Whatever the explanation for these photos of my father and Juliette together, I won't go back on my decision. I tell myself, yet again, that I don't have a choice but then I realize that actually I've always had a choice. And still do. I've chosen to give my sister a chance of survival.

I glance around the apartment one last time. So this is where the story ends. I mustn't falter, I must stay strong. And brave. Sure of myself. What I'm about to do is the most difficult thing I've done in my life. Of course it is. A gift like this is far from risk-free. I can't be sure that I'll come away unharmed, I'm very aware of that.

I go down the stairs one by one. Taking my time. A few seconds here and there won't make a difference. It's strange, this is the first time in my life that I've been so acutely aware of my own body. It's as if I can feel even the smallest shifts of fluids. The blood pulsing in my temples. The beating of my heart matches the rhythm of my footfalls almost perfectly. As I get closer to the street, the pessimism in me calms, once and for all. I force myself to see only the positives, the happiness. I say goodbye to my former life because whatever happens, I know that everything will be different from now on. Or will be over. I'm like a star at the Cannes Film Festival but instead of that famous walk up the steps, I'm walking down.

On the first stair, the taste of that ice cream shared with Marie earlier.

On the second stair, the sugary notes of Désiré's kiss.

On the third stair, my father's voice, his gentle inflection, his *I love yous*.

On the fourth stair, his smile when I came out of school and he took me in his arms, smothering me with kisses, calling me his little darling and then handing me a warm hunk of bread.

On the sixth stair, every Christmas from my childhood: the candles, the carols, the glittering tinsel, the longed-for toys. My father's smile, again and forever.

On the ninth stair, the photo of my parents. Absolutely beautiful and perfect. I've studied it so closely. And loved it so dearly. It will probably be the image that my mind summons at the last moment. Even if it isn't real.

On the eleventh stair, my mother. I've felt inferior to her my whole life, not worthy to be alive instead of her. This morning I've had my doubts. Perhaps there aren't dazzling, sunny people on the one hand and worse-than-nothings on the other. Perhaps my mother would have been proud of me. Who knows? Now that Juliette or I myself could be about to join her, to meet her for the first time, I wonder whether she knew. Was she aware that deep in her very core she was harbouring twin girls, perfectly identical sisters? Did she know that life would separate them? How did she envisage her life with them? I'm sure she would have loved us, both of us. Unconditionally. I'm sure she knew. I'm convinced of it.

On the last stair, Juliette's smile. It will be back. With or without me. It will brighten the days of wonderful people. It will shine three times more brightly because there will be three of us bringing it into being.

As I reach the entrance hall of the building I feel my phone vibrate.

Unknown number.

I pick up.

And open the door at the same time.

The sounds and images collide. Such a cacophony that I struggle to grasp what really matters.

I concentrate, screwing up my eyes to help me see better and hear better.

I clearly identify a voice on the phone. It's about Juliette.

Something's happened to Juliette.

No, it's not that, quite the opposite. Juliette's about to go into the operating theatre.

They've found . . . They've found . . . This is impossible. It's miraculous.

I start to shake.

And there's an incomprehensible sight in front of me.

Madame Racine standing there. Crying.

And next to her, with her head lowered, a familiar figure. She looks up and her face is devastated too. Madame Lebrun is here in Avignon. In tears.

I don't understand what's going on at all.

I look harder.

Madame Lebrun is holding what looks like a file, clutching it to her chest. She hands it to me slowly. She's shaking too.

I start to move my phone away from my ear, ask the woman on the other end to wait a moment. I've never been good at multitasking.

I read what's written on the front of the file Madame Lebrun is holding.

And suddenly understand everything.

I understand the lies. The silence. The photos.

I understand there's no such thing as a miracle.

I cling to that file with all my strength. And collapse in slow motion against Madame Racine's and Madame Lebrun's legs.

THAT DEATH

When I found out Juliette was ill something broke inside me. Irreparably. She'd managed to hide her illness from everyone around her, her nearest and dearest. But I wasn't really one of them so she was less cautious with me. One day she took a call in front of me. She was careful to move away and speak quietly but I heard her say the time of an appointment. And the place. Saturday 11 July at the pulmonology department of the Hôpital Nord. I'd heard her coughing in the last few months, everyone had, but she'd brushed it off with a flick of her hand and a laugh. Nothing serious, everything was fine. I probably wanted to believe her. When she hung up that day, though, there was something uncharacteristically serious about her. It startled me, naturally. I didn't say anything at the time but on Saturday 11 July I followed her through the corridors of the Hôpital Nord in Marseilles.

I was the one who saw her emerge, devastated, from the consulting room of the head of pulmonology. I slipped away discreetly but I couldn't stop myself doing something. I couldn't leave her in that state. I had to be a father to her, for once in my life. To console my daughter in distress. So I pretended to bump into her by chance in the reception area, telling her that a relation of mine was in hospital with a broken hip. She couldn't lie to me, she was in tears. We sat down together and drank hospital coffee with too much sugar in it. I put my arms around her for the first time, and she told me everything: the pulmonary fibrosis, the news she'd just been given that it had rapidly deteriorated, the urgent need for a transplant . . . and the secrecy. 'You're the only person who knows, Monsieur Joseph. I would never have told you if we hadn't met here. No one else must ever know. Not Marie, not my parents. You must promise me you won't tell anyone, you won't make any reference to my illness, ever.'

I promised. I was lying. To save her.

I came home to Paris, poleaxed by the shock.

Juliette could die. And soon. Very soon. I would lose her all over again. I just couldn't. I thought of Marie, your mother, and Marie, your niece, and the two images merged – I had to find a way to alter the course of fate. The person who deserved to die wasn't Juliette at all. It was me. I know that I stole Juliette's life from her. I stole both your lives from you. The time had come to compensate, but not with minor acts like a bookshop and a child's name, with something much more important. Until then I'd always felt it would be inconceivable to reveal my true identity. I was afraid of disrupting Juliette's stability and happiness. But things were different now: Juliette's family would tolerate my posthumous intrusion if its aim was to save her. I felt sure of that. And I still do. In any event, I was being given an opportunity to make amends for real, to give life to Juliette for a second time. And to bring the two of you together at last.

Romane, I don't know whether you'll have the strength to forgive me. I've written this diary for you. I wanted you to know, I don't want to hide anything any more. I've been lying for too long but I didn't have it in me to tell you all this to your face; I couldn't have looked you in the eye. I couldn't have coped with seeing your love wither and fade. I love you with all my soul. I'm proud of you. You're my only success. And my dearest love in the last thirty-nine years. You're beautiful. You're intelligent, talented, funny and incredibly strong. Never question that. I'll always be there somewhere for you. And in your heart, I hope.

Suzanne – who you still call Madame Lebrun after all this time, and who's probably standing in front of you now – has been much more than a friend to me for many years. I know you suspected something. She was with me when I was struggling; she gave me the support I needed, and I told her about my life. My whole life. She's had her share of suffering too. So our two breeds of pain kept each other company. She was the one who encouraged me to look for Juliette twenty years ago. And now, twenty years later, when I told her what I was planning, that I wanted to save Juliette, she listened to me. She accepted my decision, even though it broke her own heart. So she helped me. What I wanted more than anything else was for you and Juliette to meet. I knew you'd love each other to bits from the moment you saw each other. I knew that you, Romane, would need support when you were told that I was dead, I wanted you to project yourself into another life, to dig yourself out of your loneliness. What could be better than an unhoped-for sister just starting out on her second life if you too were to embark on a new life? And I don't think I could ever have forgiven myself if I hadn't given you an opportunity to meet and love each other. Deep down I'd always nurtured the hope of seeing you together. Suzanne played out the scene – brilliantly, it seems – that she and I had written for you, pointing you towards the Hôpital Nord. And once you got there you managed all on your own. Otherwise we'd have helped you, of course.

I knew I could give Juliette my lungs. I'm a doctor, by training at least. I know the risks and the impossibilities. Even with the best will in the world, a parent and child aren't necessarily compatible for organ donation. I've always wanted to protect you, whatever the cost, you know that. A few years ago when you had that terrible bout of renal colic that paralysed you for days on end, I imagined the worst – you know what I'm like. I thought about offering you a kidney if it came to that. That's no ordinary gift but then my life's never been ordinary and neither have my fears. So, without telling you, I did some tests for immunological compatibility between us. The tests showed that we're compatible and because Juliette is your identical twin, I'm also compatible with Juliette. I'm sixty-five, I've never smoked, I'm in very good health so I'm sure my lungs can keep going for many years. And – officially and legally – I'd be an anonymous donor for Juliette.

I was devastated by our painful confrontation last Sunday, horrified that I'd struck you. When I realized that you were questioning whether I was your father and you conjured the image of your mother's reproach towards me . . . it was too much for me. I couldn't listen to those words, I had to stop them. I'll hate myself for it until the very end. I lied to you that day, yet again, to avoid awakening any suspicion of my grim intention. I hope you'll find a way to understand me some day.

Then I realized that you'd gone back to Avignon, but I couldn't get hold of you. You didn't answer my messages. With no news of you I was crippled with anxiety. I couldn't go to the bookshop in person because I wasn't sure I'd find you there and I couldn't take the risk. If you'd worked it all out, you would have tried to stop me doing what I have to do. It would have made it even harder, for all of us. Suzanne couldn't run the risk either so I confided in Madame Racine.

Madame Racine is a friend, we met at the bookshop about ten years ago. I was instantly captivated by her eccentricity: her flamboyant baroque outfits, her choice never to reveal her first name and to use that pseudonym as an homage to her favourite dramatist, and the way she dropped little snippets of poetic happiness into books. The last of those was for you; I've always loved that poem by Marguerite Yourcenar and I thought it was perfectly appropriate for the situation. Utterly beautiful, full of hope, and life too. When I met Madame Racine I was immediately aware of how alone she was. We would meet up outside the bookshop too – all above board, of course – and became good friends. I never told her the exact nature of my faults but I knew that, when the time came, she'd understand too. I had no choice. I needed to know where you were and where Juliette was. Madame Racine only saw one of you at the bookshop and couldn't find the other. But the Juliette she saw was strange, slightly awkward with her customers and – most significantly – she didn't recognize Madame Racine. That Juliette wasn't Juliette. When I understood what the two of you were up to with this incredible swap that you'd set up, I was absolutely terrified.

I know you, Romane. I know you so well. I knew it was a dangerous situation. I knew that your mind – which is as twisted as mine – could alight on the idea of sacrifice, but I didn't know exactly what Juliette had told you. So I went to see her in hospital two days ago. Her condition had deteriorated and she couldn't talk but she'd written letters for her parents, for Marie and for you. Your sister's an incredible woman, Romane. She'd also worked out that if you knew she didn't have cancer but fibrosis, you'd contemplate what for her was unconscionable: risking your life for the sake of hers. So she lied to you and mentioned cancer. It was a half-lie because that was indeed one of the possibilities explored in the last few weeks. She wanted to protect you.

I knew you'd been to the hospital too when your phone calls got more persistent last night. Then when you arranged to meet me in Marseilles I knew what you were planning, and I knew you wouldn't give up, you'd see it through. So I needed to act quickly, the time had come.

It's up to me and me alone to save Juliette. I don't want to take any risks with your life, Romane. I considered that option too, making organ donations together in perfect unity. But it's an extremely rare procedure, and it takes a lot of forward planning with ethical screening to check that there are strong enough ties between the donors and the recipient. There's no guarantee that our circumstances would have been viewed favourably in the screening process. A repentant father who abandoned his daughter forty years earlier and a twin sister who has no official connection to the patient . . . it's not exactly set up for a swift and easy decision. And Juliette had very little time.

I knew that tonight would be the last time I heard your voice.

I was already in Marseilles, everything was ready. I was waiting for the right moment, the signal.

I will leave this world today with a heart full of happiness.

I'm leaving behind all the lies. I need to break away from them now. I ask your forgiveness, Romane, yet again. I ask you both to forgive me. For everything. For your lives and for my death.

My heart is calm now because, although I've never believed in the hereafter, now that I'm about to take this great step I'm wondering whether I might be reunited with your mother. That would be so wonderful. I'm clinging to that thought. And to a mental picture of you two, my daughters, together for the rest of your lives.

You still have so much life to live, and to share.

Live and be happy, my darlings, my queens.

I love you both.

Dad

25

The girls

The pain is immeasurable.

I don't think I've ever felt anything like it.

I have to force myself to think of something else. Steer my brain away from the agony. Terrible agony.

Images spool by at great speed. Or, to be more accurate, they spool by slowly. I have plenty of time to see them.

Memory is a peculiar thing. The first image that comes back to me, the one that will always be engraved on my retina, is one I never saw. One I invented. A slick death. With no splatter of blood. Celestial. Pure. Cruelly beautiful, devastatingly so. My father. Offering his last breath and every breath to come to his second daughter.

The pain returns. Stronger still. Indescribable.

Another image. Two women in tears. Two loving, protective women. Two admirable women, whom I've come to know better. Experiencing something like this together establishes a hell of a bond. An indestructible bond. Madame Racine's tears, Suzanne Lebrun's sobs. The precise moment where their pain mingles – I think that's a beautiful image too.

I can't move any more. I'm confronting myself, using my last resources, the last of my strength. I hold back my screams, ball my fists.

I can see Juliette, the incredulity on her ghostly white face when she opened her eyes and saw me there in front of her surrounded by her family. The family that had lied to her all those years. Out of love, too much love. The family that Juliette forgave instantly, unconditionally, or with just one condition: that they should continue to love each other just as much and there should be no change in their relationship. The family that immediately included me, accepted me and loved me. The family I now belong to. Just when I have no other. And I'm now the second daughter, the one who was abandoned, aged thirty-nine.

I can see Juliette. Her fight to get back to a normal life. A long, difficult fight. We would never have guessed it would be so long and so difficult. But Juliette is here, she's very much here. Her life is back to what it was before. No, it's better than before. Fuller. With a different feel to it. Tastes, sounds, depth of colour . . . everything is amplified. Juliette lives more intensely. And I actually live rather than just existing. We're survivors. We were born a second time on that Saturday in 2015. The doctors have told Juliette her breathing is like a young woman's. We all know it's the breathing of a man in his sixties. By the time the hospital understood how we were all connected it was already too late. The harm had been done. The good had been done. Or what our father wanted, in any event. We know that, to this day, our case is still being considered by ethical authorities. In utmost secrecy, because it poses a substantial problem in a country where euthanasia is illegal. Do we have the right to choose the end of our lives? Do we have the right to choose to offer life? Isn't there a risk of encouraging generations of parents to sacrifice themselves to save their children? I don't think so. Our case is exceptional. If we'd been officially recognized as a family, my father's sacrifice would have been impossible, and that's a good thing. I'm convinced that organ donation should remain anonymous. Attitudes are improving, more and more people register as donors. And I'm sure that within a matter of years, scientific and medical progress will mean artificial organs can be transplanted. History ploughs forward.

I scream. A great long scream that tears through the room. I don't know how to cope. I'm frightened I'll pass out. I try to regulate my breathing – which has never been my strong point.

I feel a surge of euphoria through my bloodstream as I think back over what Juliette and I have experienced since then. We had thirty-nine years to catch up on, so we decided to describe them to each other, in detail. Juliette closed her bookshop in Avignon, I closed my practice in Paris and we went away, just the two of us, for three weeks in a little chalet in the middle of the Alps. We took along photos and all sorts of other things that meant something to us – some of them profound but many of them superficial and trivial. Three weeks, just her and me. We devoted the first two days to exploring our family story, the stories of our parents, the birth ones and the adoptive ones. Later we threw ourselves body and soul into the Nineties, putting on fluorescent leggings, dancing to Madonna, Prince, George Michael, the Cranberries and Ace of Base. We laughed uproariously reading back through forgotten pages of our teenage diaries, and tracking the progress of Juliette's changing hairstyles across the years. We cried a lot too about everything we hadn't shared, all those snippets of childhood we would never have together. Those three weeks were among the most intense of my life. A life, I now realize, that's only just beginning.

But right now I feel as if I'm dying.

It shouldn't be possible to be in such agony, not in the twenty-first century. People keep telling me that it's normal for it to hurt. And I have to say, it was my choice. I now regret that decision but it's too late to rewind. I feel a stabbing pain like a dagger inside. I grit my teeth.

And grab Désiré's hand.

He's here beside me, encouraging me. Even at two o'clock in the morning, even in the white glare of hospital strip lights, he's so gorgeous that I get an urge to slap him just so he can be in pain too. After all, he's as responsible as I am for what I'm going through. I do nothing of the sort, obviously. I do snap a few insults at him, though, I think.

I take a deep breath and bellow out a scream. Désiré follows the instructions he's been given to the letter. A spritz of water from an atomizer into my mouth, pant like a dog, encouragement, let's push.

I'm dying.

No, I'm alive.

I think about my mother. About what she endured alone on New Year's Day 1976. I drive away the mental pictures because they've haunted me ever since I've known, and now isn't the time.

I conjure up a different image, a more beautiful, more dazzling one.

When my father died I had to sort through and file or throw away everything he'd collected over the course of his life, including things he'd deliberately hidden from me all those years. When I was moving a suitcase that had belonged to my mother and now contained photos of her childhood, it slipped from my grasp. It was too heavy and fell to the floor, slightly ripping its lining. I automatically slid my hand inside. I always do this when I'm emptying a bag: I run my hand all over it to check I haven't missed anything.

I stopped dead. Stunned. My hand had found something. A thin sheet of paper. A letter written by my mother.

I sat down and started reading.

And immediately felt sure I was the first person who'd ever laid eyes on this letter. My father didn't know about it.

If he'd read this letter, he would have mentioned it in the file he left for me the day he died.

If he'd read this letter, he might not have made the same decisions. If he'd read this letter, our lives might well have been very different. What a waste . . .

I push harder, and harder still. Désiré is panting next to me and I feel as if my jaws will shatter if I keep grinding them like this. The midwife reassures me, that's very good, Romane, you're doing really well. How old is she? Twenty-two? What does she know about the agony of childbirth? *Let's talk about this when you've decided to give birth naturally, with no epidural, the good old-fashioned way, and all because I told myself I had to stop giving in to my fears. Never again, Romane.* In this particular instance, I'd have done better to listen to my anxieties.

In her letter, my mother talks to us, to her unborn children.

Judging by the handwritten date, this improbable letter was written when my mother was four months pregnant. And it answered the question I'd asked myself on the last day of my father's life. Did my mother know she was carrying twins?

She didn't, her words make that very clear. She couldn't have known.

But it was what she hoped for.

Her letter is addressed to 'the girls'. Her daughters. My mother was convinced she would have two girls. Perhaps not both at once, she didn't mention that, but she dreamed of these two daughters.

In the letter she describes her ideal world and her ideal family. She describes them very poetically, very sensitively, her writing expansive and assured, with no extraneous flourishes but well-chosen words and a sort of literary momentum that sat well with the image I'd always had of her.

There would be two daughters in my mother's ideal family. She would love them to distraction. Joseph would love them to distraction. And they would love each other to distraction. She would introduce them to the pleasures of reading and theatre because that was what she herself loved. And they might tend towards medicine, you never know, if Joseph insisted. She would call them Romane and Juliette. Shakespearian names without the attendant tragedy. Those were her very words. Devastating. Life could have been so wonderful with her.

I push again, for longer, and much harder.

All at once everyone shouts. They can see her head.

'She's here, Romane.'

Then I hear her cry and I dissolve in tears. I lose all notion of time.

Moments later, but it feels like an eternity to me, I'm holding my daughter in my arms. Gently nestled against my heart.

I study her and instinctively know my world will never be the same again. I glance at Désiré. He's in tears too. He tells me she's perfect, he's sure she is, even though he can't see her.

Suddenly, the pain comes again.

Just as intense. Just as powerful. Or worse even, I can't tell. My daughter's crying encourages me.

I've never felt so invincible. So happy to be alive.

I give a guttural, instinctive wail. A cry from my very depths.

My whole life and all the deaths associated with it are contained in that cry.

I close my eyes. Let my tears flow. Slowly.

I keep crushing Désiré's hand and suddenly I hear her. My whole body relaxes. I stop crying.

Open my eyes.

And that's when I see her.

Squirming in Désiré's arms. Just as beautiful as I pictured her.

Longed for. Luminous. Amazing. Restorative.

My second daughter.

ACKNOWLEDGEMENTS

The past year has been incredible. A whirlwind of happiness, surprises, discoveries and new faces. And there are so many people to thank . . .

First of all, thank you to my editor extraordinaire, Caroline Lépée. Thank you for your support, for our discussions, for your ideas and comments, your questions that sometimes shake me up, often encourage me, help me move forward and improve my writing. I'm ridiculously lucky to work with you. And there are plenty more drinks together to come.

Thank you to Philippe Robinet for the ever-open door, the attentive ear, the 'ban bourguignon' songs and your enduring faith in me that moves me far more than I let it show.

Thank you to the whole team at Calmann-Lévy for really getting behind *La Chambre des Merveilles* (*The Book of Wonders*). Without your wonderful work my first novel would never have had such a 'surreal' destiny . . . I'm fully aware of that. Particular thanks to Patricia

Roussel and Julia Balcells who propelled our beloved kawaii cat far beyond what we'd hoped. To Christelle Pestana, Adeline Vanot, Antoine Lebourg, Sarah Altenloh and Fanny Plan who involved many journalists, bloggers and literary event organizers in the adventure. Thank you to Camille Lucet, the quinoa queen and high priestess of book-launch programmes; to Virginie Ebat and the Hachette marketing teams for their invaluable work with bookshops. Thank you to Catherine Bourgey, Anne Sitruk, Mélanie Trapateau, Chloé Herla, Margaux Poujade and all the others who make their offices feel (almost) like home.

Thank you to the booksellers who supported me from the start: I can't name everyone but I'd like to thank specifically Gérard Collard, Lydie Zannini, Caroline Vallat, Philippe Fournier, Amandine Ardouin, Stanislas Rigot, Antoine Bonnet, Sandrine Dantard and also Nadège, Alice, Yohann, Céline . . . thank you, all of you.

Thank you to the journalists who liked my first novel and said so, headed up by Bernard Lehut whose 'blurb' has already been translated into Italian, Japanese and Icelandic!

Thank you to the many bloggers, commentators and Instagrammers who supported *The Book of Wonders*, with a special mention for Emilie 'Bulledop', Ophélie, Jenna, Bénédicte, Margaux, Karine and Yvan.

Thank you to Professor Françoise Le Pimpec Barthes

and doctors Reger Bessis and Nicolas Peron for taking the time to answer my sometimes outlandish medical questions, and to Denis Chofflet for his clarifications about public records.

Thank you to my family. Mathilde, Alessandro and Éléonore, you are my foundations, my anchor, my indispensables. Without you nothing would taste or feel the same. You carry me forwards, always and forever. Thank you to my parents, Muriel and Serge, for giving me enough love and confidence to believe nothing is really impossible – Dad, of course you can keep working as a local press officer. To Alexandre and Andréa: I thought about you a lot when I wrote this story about the love between two sisters, who could have been three brothers. Floriane, Fanny, Jules, Noé, André, Raphaèle, Pierre, thank you for reading and for your animated comments about titles and covers, your positive waves and all the good times we've shared – March 2018 was particularly full of happy times. Thank you to my grandfather Pascal and to my family in Hyères and elsewhere (a nod and a wink to team N.), for being by my side.

Last but not least, thank you to you, my readers, who write to me, come to see me, or simply share your enthusiasm for what I write. You can't imagine how much the things you say move me and encourage me to keep going. Thank you from the bottom of my heart.

Julien